ENDLESS MIDNIGHT

The Moonlight Breed 5

Gabrielle Evans

MENAGE EVERLASTING
MANLOVE

Siren Publishing, Inc.
www.SirenPublishing.com

A SIREN PUBLISHING BOOK
IMPRINT: Ménage Everlasting ManLove

ENDLESS MIDNIGHT
Copyright © 2011 by Gabrielle Evans

ISBN-10: 1-61926-307-6
ISBN-13: 978-1-61926-307-9

First Printing: December 2011

Cover design by Jinger Heaston
All cover art and logo copyright © 2011 by Siren Publishing, Inc.

Printed in the U.S.A.

PUBLISHER
Siren Publishing, Inc.
www.SirenPublishing.com

ENDLESS MIDNIGHT

The Moonlight Breed 5

GABRIELLE EVANS

Prologue

"We're not going to get out of here alive are we?" Boston huddled in the corner of the dank basement on the scrap of blanket that doubled as his bed. He curled against his mate's side for warmth as his nude body shivered from the cold.

For three years, he'd endured the desolation of his prison. The only thing that had kept him going was Flynn. While he would have preferred to meet his mate under more welcoming circumstances, he was just happy to have Flynn Murphy at his side.

"We're gonna be fine," Flynn said in his sexy Irish accent.

Boston adored that accent, and it made his cock hard every time Flynn spoke. It had been hell the first two years after he'd met Flynn. With the man being three years his senior, and Boston only sixteen when he'd been sold to the vampire coven by his family, Flynn had refused to touch him. Now he was nineteen, though, and things were different.

He hated when the vampires manipulated their minds and forced them together for their sick enjoyment. It still made something in his stomach cramp that their first time together had been with several of the bloodsuckers watching their every movement. They had taken the most special moment in Boston's young life and turned it into something cheap and sleazy.

Normally, however, he craved Flynn's touch. It was like a soothing balm to his frayed and delicate psyche after the horrors he was forced to live with day in and day out.

Crawling into Flynn's lap to straddle his hips, Boston licked at his mate's mouth and grinned. "I love you, Flynn Murphy."

"Aye, and I love you, Boston Mackey. Let me show you. Be mine forever."

Boston shook his head sadly. He had no illusions that he'd survive the hell they were in. As bonded mates, they literally couldn't live without each other. He wouldn't tie them together just so Flynn could die. The big Irish shifter was stronger than him, so maybe he'd have a chance to escape. Boston wouldn't risk his mate by claiming him if there was any way Flynn could be free of the awful place.

Flynn sighed, andhis strong fingers wrapped around Boston's hard cock where it throbbed between them, leaking against Flynn's belly, and all thoughts fled.

It took only minutes for the stroke of Flynn's tongue against his and the steady rhythm of his hand to bring Boston to completion. Groaning quietly, he stared into Flynn's green eyes, watching the dim candlelight flicker there before tumbling over the edge and spilling his seed into Flynn's hand.

God, he was so tired. The vampires who held them as blood slaves—and sometimes more—kept them so drained that Boston couldn't even shift. On the full moons when he had no control over his transformations, the vampires locked him inside a steel box, barely big enough for his stag to fit until he'd changed back to his human form.

Flynn held him tightly to his chest, stroking his spine and whispering kisses over his temple. "Sleep now, darlin'."

Boston didn't know when he'd finally fallen asleep, but he woke, cold and alone, curled up on the raggedy blanket. A shuffling sound drew his attention, and he scrambled back into the corner, praying it wasn't one of the bloodsuckers up for an early morning snack. Damn, he hated when they drank from him.

Curious when the sound didn't come closer, he easedout of his corner and toward thehuge support beam. Pressing against the wood, he peeked around the corner. What he saw made his stomach cramp and his heart shatter into a million pieces.

That answered his question of where Flynn was.

Hurrying back to his corner, he moved as far away from his makeshift bed as possible, kneeling and gagging on the cement floor, before finally expelling the meager contents of his stomach. God, he'd been so stupid!

Wiping his mouth on the back of his hand, he crawled to his blanket and curled into a fetal position, squeezing his eyes closed against the pain. A long time later, he felt Flynn's warm body mold to his back, and Boston couldn't stop himself from stiffening. Apparently, Flynn noticed because he eased back to put space between them, and never spoke a word.

The next time Boston woke, it was to a hand fisted in his hair and two sets of fangs embedded in his neck. He screamed and kicked, bucking his body and trying to get a way. This was it. They were going to kill him.

Part of him hoped they did. He was already dead on the inside after Flynn's betrayal. No one would notice, no one would care if he never came back. *God, just please let me die.*

He didn't die, though. He passed out and regained consciousness several times as the vampires tied a rope around his ankles and dragged his limp body out into the night. The first time he'd been outside in more than three years, and he could barely open his eyes to enjoy it.

The bloodsuckers dragged him along by the rope through several inches of bitterly cold snow, and the next thing Boston knew, he was being hoisted upside down. He dangled several feet above the ground, his legs protesting his weight as the rope cut into the flesh of his ankles.

He swung there until morning, then through the day. Thankfully, he slept—or something close to sleep—throughout most of it. When the night came again, he woke to something jarring the ropes holding him up in the tree.

Maybe it was the vampires back to finish him off. He didn't care. He welcomed death. No one could live through the pain he was in, both emotionally and physically, and he just prayed for it to end.

Strong arms wrapped around his midsection, lowering him to the ground and holding him close to a warm, muscled chest. *Flynn.* No matter what the man had done to him, he loved him. He wanted Flynn—needed him.

"Can you, hear me?"

Boston frowned. That wasn't Flynn. With a great deal of effort, he blinked open his eyes and stared up at the biggest man he'd ever seen. He was a little fuzzy around the edges, but Boston knew he'd never met the guy before.

Another man stood beside him, and still another was kneeling in the snow, holding Boston in his lap. "Who are you?" *Was that his voice?* He sounded like he'd been gargling glass. And why did it matter who they were? They were probably going to kill him as well. He didn't need to know their names to understand that.

Who just stomped around in the woods at night with honorable intentions? All the childhood stories he had heard were true. There really were monsters that lurked in the night. He'd lived with them for years. These were just a different kind.

"I'm Xander Brighton," the biggest man answered with a nod. "You're safe now. Everything is going to be okay."

Boston's head lolled against the shoulder supporting him without his permission. He just couldn't seem to keep it up. "Nothing will ever be okay again."

Chapter One

Eight years later…

Boston was tired, pissed off, and freezing his fucking nuts off. He'd driven across the damn country, been attacked by a bloodsucker, and now he was expected to go tromping through the woods in the middle of a blizzard to rescue someone he'd never even met. Yep, life was just damn peachy.

A commotion outside his small room in the cabin drew his attention. "What now?" he grumbled under his breath as he went to investigate. Stepping out of the room, he froze in his tracks when five men shuffled into the cabin behind Xander and Talon. He immediately recognized them as the assholes who'd attacked their pack at the diner. "What the fuck are they doing here?" he yelled. Had his alpha completely lost his mind?

Xander held up his hands, palms out. He looked wary and just a little pissed off at Boston's attitude. "They're here to help. Calm down, and let's hear what they have to say."

What choice did he have? Nodding curtly, he crossed his arms over his chest, glaring at the vampires and prepared to defend his family by any means necessary. While anger boiled just under the surface, deeper inside, Boston trembled with fear. The sooner they could get the bloodsuckers out of there, the better.

His eyes strayed to the smallest of the group as the head vampire went through his introductions. The guy was damn sexy for a vampire, but there was something else about him that wouldn't allow Boston to look away.

"This is Malakai, the tech man, and kind of liaison of sorts," the leader, Stavion, finished.

Malakai lifted his eyes, looking straight at Boston, and Boston felt his brain go fuzzy, his gums itch, and his belly flutter. What the hell was going on? Then everything seemed to come in slow motion as the small man crossed the room to stand directly in front of him.

His sweet scent hit Boston like a runaway freight train, slamming into him hard enough to steal the air from his lungs. His nostrils flared, his cock hardened, and his blood roared inside his ears. *Mine!*

That one thought brought Boston out of his lusty haze, and he stumbled back, shaking his head frantically. "I will not have a vampire as a mate!" Without another word, he spun around and raced for the sanctuary of the bedroom. Slamming the door closed behind him, he fell to his knees and began pulling at his hair. "Not again," he whimpered. Fate was the cruelest bitch he'd ever met.

He could hear the others talking in the next room, but he couldn't make out what they were saying. Struggling up from the floor, he staggered over to the bed and perched on the edge of the mattress. His *sienota* could not be a vampire. He refused to accept it.

Just like your first mate refused to accept you, an evil voice whispered inside his head. *You're so broken not even your mate wants you.* "Damn it," Boston growled.

The bedroom door creaked open, and Keeton strolled in with a wide smile on his face. The little vampire shuffled in behind him, his head lowered and his eyes downcast.

"Get him out!" Boston roared. He couldn't be in the same room with the man without wanting to pounce on him and lick every inch of his skin. He wouldn't do it, though. He couldn't.

"Oh, shut up already," Braxton said sourly as he followed in behind the other two. "We're right here, and we're not fucking deaf." He slammed the door hard enough to shake the walls, crossed his arms over his chest, and glared. "You're being a complete dick," he added in a quieter voice.

"I'm sorry," Malakai whispered. "I'll go."

Keeton wound his arm around the vampire's shoulders and held him in place. Boston bit back his growl before it could escape. He didn't like Keeton touching his mate. No one should be touching Malakai except him. Only, he couldn't, and he knew it.

"Why are you so against being his mate?" Braxton asked.

"That's really none of your business." Boston jumped up from the bed and moved across the room, as far as he could get from Malakai.

"Well, I think it's his business," Keeton said with a dip of his head toward the vampire beside him.

"It's okay. I understand." Malakai still spoke in that same dejected whisper that ripped at Boston's heart.

"I can't." Boston pleaded for the man to hear him. "I'm sorry, but I can't."

Malakai held his hands up and shook his head. "Please, just stop. I get it."

Oh, he really didn't, but Boston wasn't going to argue with him. They all stood in silence for a long time, not even Braxton or Keeton speaking. Boston felt like he was suffocating. They were too close. *Malakai* was too close. He needed to get away.

Maybe it made him a coward, but that's exactly what he intended to do—run away and never look back.

* * * *

Jackson's brother rescued, his father in custody, and evidence collected, Boston was damn glad to be going home. He'd worked his ass off all week to do everything in his power to get them the hell out of Wyoming.

He hadn't seen Malakai again, but the man consumed his thoughts. Maybe more distance would help him forget that the man ever existed.

"So, when is this Enforcer guy supposed to be here?" Braxton asked as they bumped along the long, winding driveway that would lead them home.

Boston sat up straighter in his seat, waiting to hear Xander's answer. He'd been hiding out from everyone, and this was the first he'd heard that anyone was coming to live with them.

"Flynn's supposed to be here next Saturday. I guess he can stay in Jackson's old room now that Talon's finally pulled his head out of his ass."

The name made Boston's gut clench, and he felt the blood drain from his face. He was being ridiculous, though. It couldn't be the same Flynn.

"I'll make sure it's clean and put new sheets on the bed. How long is he staying?"

Xander shrugged as he pulled to a stop behind Logan's Jeep. "I guess as long as Blaise feels it's necessary. Flynn is supposed to be one of the best, and if keeping you safe means having him here, then I won't complain."

Braxton smiled sweetly and leaned over the console to kiss his mate. Boston looked away. Not because he was embarrassed, but because he felt ashamed. He could have that, but he'd thrown it away.

"Flynn Murphy," Braxton mused when he pulled away from Xander's lips. "Is he Irish?"

Boston was out of the truck and running toward the back of the house before Xander could answer. Yes, Flynn Murphy was definitely Irish, and the most gorgeous man Boston had ever laid eyes on. Too bad the asshole didn't want him.

Stripping out of his clothes as he ran, he stopped just inside the tree line and forced himself to calm down enough to shift. Once his buck had taken over, Boston forced his brain to shut down and ran. He didn't have a destination, had no clue where he was going, but he ran until he couldn't feel his legs anymore.

Folding his tired limbs beneath him, Boston curled up on the ground and closed his eyes. Maybe if he was lucky he'd wake up and find it had all been some horrible nightmare.

Unfortunately, he'd never been that lucky.

* * * *

The following Saturday, Boston woke to the sounds of laughter. Blinking against the light spilling in through his bedroom window, he forced himself out of bed and dressed in a daze. If Flynn was going to be living with them, he couldn't avoid the man forever. It would be better to face the situation head-on as though nothing was wrong. The last thing he needed was for his pack mates to start asking questions.

Pulling his shirt over his head, he padded out of the room in his bare feet and down the hall to the stairs.

"Aye, I'm from Ireland. Does that get ya hot and bothered?" Flynn's voice floated up to Boston, and he gripped the railing to keep from tumbling down the stairs.

"It better not," Logan growled.

Keeton laughed. "Ooh, you know I love it when you're jealous."

"Boston!" Braxton shouted.

Plastering a smile on his face that he didn't feel, Boston navigated the remainder of the stairs and stepped into the living room. "Hey," he said lamely. He did enjoy watching Flynn's face pale a little too much, though. At least the big Irishman was just as affected as Boston.

Flynn rose slowly from where he'd been sitting on the sofa. "Hello, Boston."

Boston dipped his head. "Flynn."

"You two know each other?" Jackson looked back and forth between them with his eyebrows drawn together.

"We've met," Boston answered vaguely. "It's been a long time," he said to Flynn.

"Aye, that it has. Ya look good."

Boston snorted. It was a damn lie, and he knew it. Since meeting

Malakai he'd barely slept, the mere thought of food turned his stomach, and it showed in his smaller body mass and the dark circles under his eyes. "Thanks."

"Maybe we should leave you two alone." Talon jerked his head toward the kitchen, indicating everyone should follow him.

"No," Boston said to stop them. "I just wanted to greet our guest. I'm going back to bed."

"Are you going to work tonight?" Talon asked.

"I'll be there." Before he could do something to make a complete fool out of himself, Boston turned around and hurried back up the stairs. Jogging down the hall, he reached the relative safety of his room and sighed. "I can't do this."

He'd never considered leaving the pack, but maybe he could find a place to stay until Flynn's guard duty was up and he'd moved on.

"Boston?"

Fuck, fuck, fuck! It wouldn't do for Flynn to know how upset he was. He wouldn't give the man that kind of power over him. Gathering his composure, he opened his door and looked into his mate's deep green eyes. "Hey, Flynn. What's up?"

"We should talk."

"I don't really think we have anything to say to each other."

"That's not true, and ya bloody well know it. Stop bein' a damn fool, and let me in."

Boston shook his head sadly. "I let you in once before, and we both know how that ended. I have no intentions of repeating past mistakes."

"It ended with ya runnin' off in the middle of the night. Care to explain that one?"

"What does it matter to you? You didn't want me. I was broken, and you just couldn't be bothered."

Flynn's eyes narrowed and his lips pressed into a thin line. "That's rubbish, and ya know it, Boston Mackey. What happened to ya?"

"You happened, and now Malakai," Boston whispered.

"Who's Malakai?" The slight growl in Flynn's voice made Boston shiver, but he refused to acknowledge the attraction.

"My mate."

"I am your mate!" Flynn's fist pounded against the doorframe.

"Well, apparently, I have two. I guess that means he's your mate as well." Boston didn't have a damn clue why he was telling the man this. Maybe he hoped if Flynn knew about Malakai he'd go find the little vampire, and they'd both just leave Boston alone.

Flynn seemed to calm a little, and the corners of his mouth actually twitched. "So, where is this mate of ours?"

"In Wyoming."

Flynn's brow wrinkled in confusion. "Now, why would he be there?"

"He's a vampire." Boston said it as though that explained everything, and in a way, it did.

"Oh, babe," Flynn breathed. He reached out to touch Boston's cheek, but Boston jerked away and shook his head.

"Don't make this harder for me. Please, just leave me alone." He didn't like begging, but if that's what it took to protect his heart, he'd do it on his knees in a sea of broken glass. He wouldn't let Flynn Murphy in again. Not this time.

"Ya always were stubborn." Flynn sounded proud of the fact. He smirked crookedly and winked. "I'll wear ya down yet, Boston Mackey."

Boston didn't say a word as he closed the door quietly in the man's handsome face. If he was being honest, that was exactly what he was afraid would happen. He'd never had any resistance to Flynn. Why did he think he could start now?

Chapter Two

"Hello, sweetheart," Flynn purred when Boston walked into the kitchen. Oh, he loved seeing the angry look in his mate's eyes. In the nearly three months he'd been there, it was the only time he received any kind of fucking emotion from Boston.

"Go to hell," Boston shot back.

Braxton groaned and let his head drop forward until his brow banged against the table. "Could you guys give it a rest for five goddamn minutes? Please? I'm begging. I've never seen mates act like this."

Flynn sighed but refrained from any further taunting. He knew it wasn't fair to the other men in the house. Hell, he didn't even know why he did it. He supposed it was because he wanted to see something in Boston's eyes when he looked at him besides…nothing. That's when Boston bothered to look at him at all. Most of the time, he did everything in his power to avoid being in the same room as Flynn.

He opened his mouth to apologize to Braxton, but before he could say anything, Keeton came skidding into the room, almost plowing into Boston's back. "Jackson's on the phone with Blaise. Willow and Cole are missing."

Flynn was out of his chair and moving before he even registered the intent to do so. "Lock the doors and stay away from the windows," he commanded.

Keeton looked at him for a minute before he snorted and rolled his eyes. "You do realize that they live in Wyoming, right? Nothing has happened here since that bitch tried to eat Logan."

"That's not important. I was sent here to do a job, and I'm trying to do it."

"You're being a jackass." Keeton flicked his wrist. "Go play so I can talk to Braxton."

Flynn's hackles rose at the casual dismissal, and he felt his chest rumble with a low growl. How the hell was he supposed to protect these men when they seemed hell-bent on ignoring him?

"Flynn," Boston said quietly. He moved closer, blocking Flynn's view of Keeton. "You need to calm down or Logan's going to rip you apart, man. You should know how Keeton is by now. No one's here to hurt us."

That's when it hit him. He wasn't as upset about Keeton's dismissal as he was that there was a possible threat to his mate. Blinking several times, he took a few calming breaths and met Boston's eyes. "Right."

"So, I guess Jackson is going to Wyoming?" Braxton asked.

"He's looking for a flight now."

"Is Talon going with him?"

Keeton crossed his arms over his chest and huffed. "Logan and Xander are going, too, or so they say."

Braxton sighed and nodded in resignation. "I was afraid you'd say that. They just can't help themselves."

"Well, I'm going, too," Keeton stated defiantly.

"No, you're not," came a deep voice from the entryway.

Flynn sidestepped Boston to see Logan standing just inside the kitchen.

"You can't just expect me to stay here," Keeton argued. "I can help!"

"That's exactly what I expect. I don't want your help, I want you to be safe. Listen to Flynn and Boston. They'll keep your cute little ass out of trouble until I get back."

Flynn expected Boston to argue, to say he was going to help his friends. When his mate didn't say anything, Flynn eyed him curiously. Boston had gone completely still, and all the blood had drained from his face. His lips pressed together so tightly, they'd turned white, and he looked like he was going to be sick.

"Boston." Flynn reached out, but Boston dodged his advance as always and shook his head rapidly.

"Blaise is my cousin!" Keeton yelled. "I need to go with you."

"You need to stay here and stop arguing," Logan countered. "There's nothing you can do in Wyoming but get in the way."

Flynn knew it was the wrong thing to say the minute it left Logan's mouth. He didn't even have time to intervene before the inevitable blowup happened. Sweet Jesus, he'd never heard anyone screech like that. He was half-tempted to cover his ears. Keeton had a very vivid imagination, and quite the violent streak. Flynn wasn't sure if half of the man's threats were physically possible.

Logan didn't flinch. The man was either used to his mate's tantrums, or he had a bigger set of balls than Flynn. He wasn't even the one being yelled at, and Flynn wanted to run and duck for cover.

"You'll get used to it," Boston said out of the corner of his mouth.

Flynn knew he shouldn't read too much into it, but his heart swelled with hope that Boston's statement meant Flynn would be around long enough *to* get used to it. He had no idea what he'd done to send the young shifter running, and Boston didn't exactly seem open to conversation.

"Are you finished?" Logan asked calmly.

Keeton huffed and puffed like he'd run a mile, but he pursed his lips and nodded curtly.

Logan smiled. "Behave yourself." He bent and kissed the top of his mate's head. "I'll be back before you know it. Besides, you have a wedding to get ready for, don't you?"

Keeton squeaked, flapped his hands around his face, and hurried out of the room.

Logan laughed under his breath. "Works every time."

Within the hour, everyone was packed and loaded up in Logan's

Jeep. Keeton and Braxton were taking them to the airport, leaving Flynn alone with Boston for the first time since he'd arrived. It was what he'd been wanting—a chance to talk to his mate without interruption—so why the hell was he so nervous?

"I have to get ready for work," Boston mumbled and headed for the stairs.

"Do ya think that's a good idea?" Flynn knew Boston could take care of himself, but with the kidnapping of Cole and Willow, his protective instincts were in high gear.

"Flynn." Boston sighed. "Nothing has happened since you came here. Nothing is *going* to happen. Maybe it's time for you to move on. I'm sure Blaise can reassign you to a place where you're needed."

Keeping his face impassive, Flynn watched Boston climb the stairs and disappear from view. He wouldn't let on to how much the words hurt. Logically, he knew Boston didn't need him, but then again, there was nothing logical about his feelings for Boston.

The longer he stood there thinking about the younger man's dismissal, the more pissed off he became. It was one thing for Boston to not want him, but he felt he at least deserved an explanation.

"No," he growled and marched toward the staircase. He'd lost Boston once, and he didn't intend to do it a second time. The man would hear him out if Flynn had to tie him to the bed.

The thought of Boston tied to his bed, naked and at his mercy, had Flynn's cock swelling inside his jeans. *Shit!* Pushing away his less than virtuous thoughts, he took the stairs two at a time, stomped down the hall, and threw Boston's bedroom door open without knocking.

Stopping just inside the doorway, his chest constricted when he spotted Boston sitting on the edge of the mattress with his face buried in his hands. "Why won't you just leave me alone?"

Crossing the room, Flynn knelt on the floor in front of his mate and rested his hands on Boston's knees. "I can't do that, *mo chroí.*"

"Don't call me that." There was no heat in Boston's voice—more of a desperate pleading.

"What has ya so upset then?" *Please let me in*, he added silently.

Instead of answering, Boston scrubbed his hands over his face. Then he stood so abruptly, Flynn fell over on his ass. Boston looked down at him but didn't offer an apology. "I have to get ready for work."

"I guess that's right. If you're goin' to be a stubborn fool, then I guess I'll be comin' with ya."

"You need to stay here and watch out for Braxton and Keeton. I can take care of myself. They can't." Boston didn't even look at him as he spoke. "They'll be back within the hour, and I don't want them coming home to an empty house. They're my family. Keep them safe."

It was the first thing Boston had asked of him, and Flynn wanted to say no. However, there was no rule saying that Flynn had to protect the pipsqueaks at the house. From the minute Boston had walked down those stairs on the morning of Flynn's arrival, Flynn had promised himself that wherever Boston went was where he'd follow. Even if the younger man wouldn't acknowledge their bond, it was Flynn's instinct to want to protect his mate.

"Okay," he finally agreed. "I'll keep 'em safe."

* * * *

The music was too loud. The drinks were overpriced. The club was crowded, smoky, and suffocating. Flynn sat at a table in the far corner, asking himself again and again why he'd thought this would be a good idea.

Keeton and Braxton were enjoying themselves at least. They'd dropped by once or twice to check on him, but the majority of their time had been spent on the dance floor, gyrating their half-naked bodies with the rest of the idiots in the place.

Why anyone would want to voluntarily subject themselves to the atmosphere of Carpe Noctem was beyond him. Give him a small, local pub with a bartender who could build a perfect Guinness over this crap any day.

Keeping half his attention on the Trouble Twins, Flynn kept shooting covert glances across the room to the man moving fluidly behind the bar. Boston laughed and smiled, showing off his perfect teeth and sexy dimples. His blond hair was stylishly mussed, and the white T-shirt he wore had to be at least two sizes too small. Even from across the room, Flynn could see every dip and valley, every rippling bulge of Boston's muscles anytime the man so much as breathed.

His cock had been hard from the moment he'd caught sight of his mate. Though his temper seethed just below the surface at the way Boston flirted with the customers and allowed them to paw all over him, he couldn't tame his desire for the gorgeous bartender.

When some muscle-bound shithead grabbed the front of Boston's shirt and dragged him over the counter for a searing kiss, Flynn didn't know if he wanted to hit something or throw up. Watching Boston push the man away and laugh, Flynn thought maybe he'd do both.

"You're not going to get his attention by sitting in the corner."

Flynn looked up to see Keeton and Braxton standing in front of his table. He'd been so preoccupied with Boston, he hadn't even noticed their approach. Some great bodyguard he was.

"He doesn't want me."

"Have you given him a reason to?" Braxton asked as he slid into a seat beside Flynn. Keeton took the chair across the table and propped his elbows up on the scarred wood.

"He won't even talk to me." And why the hell was he pouring his heart out to these guys?

"Maybe you should grovel." Keeton gave a shrug and sat back in his chair. "I make Logan grovel when he screws up."

"I would kiss his arse every day of my life if I knew what the bloody hell I did wrong." Flynn slammed his beer bottle down on the table and growled.

"It doesn't matter." Braxton smiled impishly. "The point is that *he*thinks you did something wrong. Whether you did or not isn't the point. Boston has been different since Mal—uh, since Wyoming."

"I know about Malakai." That was something else he needed to discuss with Boston. If they had another mate out there, he wanted the man with him. It didn't matter to Flynn if Malakai was a vampire, a shifter, a purple rhinoceros, or a three-headed alien. A mate was a mate. If Boston wouldn't talk to him, maybe he could ask Blaise. It sounded as though the Hunter was friendly with Malakai's coven.

"Don't do it," Keeton said as though reading Flynn's mind. "You need to fix things with Boston before you even think about going after Malakai. I only met him once, but he's a good guy, and I won't let the two of you hurt him again."

"Again? What happened?" Flynn couldn't see Boston intentionally hurting anyone. *Oh,* a ghrá, *what have you done?*

"Well, he didn't beat him up or anything." Keeton sighed and rubbed at the back of his neck. "He just rejected him. Hard."

"He'll be at the wedding," Braxton added coyly.

"What? When?"

Keeton looked miffed that Flynn didn't know when his wedding to Logan was. "In four weeks."

Four weeks seemed like an excruciatingly long time. Still, the twerps had a point. He needed to make things right with Boston before he pulled Malakai into the mix. It wouldn't be fair to either of them, especially Malakai.

"Boston's shift ends in ten minutes," Braxton said, looking down at his watch. "Did you want to wait for him, or dip out and pretend like we were never here?"

Boston would be pissed if he knew Flynn had come to his place of employment just to keep an eye on him. As much as he wanted to see the man safely home, it would only cause more problems between them.

Draining the last of his beer, Flynn set the bottle on the table and stood. "Let's be goin' then."

Chapter Three

The captives were rescued, the bad guys had been brought to justice, and his best friend had gained leadership of the Redway Coven. He should be thrilled. So, why did he want to curl into a ball and die?

Boston Mackey.

For nearly two hundred years, he'd waited to find his mate, his soul's missing piece, only to find the man didn't want him. Malakai supposed he should at least be grateful that it *was* a man. He wouldn't have a clue what to do with a woman and all their soft, feminine bits.

A knock on the door had him groaning, but he eventually pushed himself into a sitting position on the side of the bed, and called for whoever waited in the hallway to enter. Unsurprised to see Stavion step into his room, Malakai groaned again and flopped to his back, throwing his arm over his face. "What do you want?"

"It's been a week since you've eaten. I'm worried about you."

"I'm fine." Malakai hated lying to his friend, but what was he supposed to tell Stavion? *"My mate doesn't want me. He's found someone else, so where does that leave me? Don't worry, though. I'd be happy to join you for tea and crumpets, and a little blood for dessert."*

Memories of the previous week still had the ability to make his stomach cramp. It wasn't Willow's fault, of course. How could the little elf know that Boston was supposed to belong to Malakai? Still, it had hurt to hear Willow carry on about the problems Boston was having with his new lover back in Georgia.

He hadn't had a single drop of blood since that day. His muscles ached, his throat felt raw, and his vision was blurry. Unfortunately, he wouldn't die from denying himself the crimson liquid he needed, but he'd feel like he was. The pain would eventually become debilitating, but maybe it would relieve him from his thoughts of Boston.

"Call him," Stavion said, and the mattress dipped beside Malakai. "Go to him. Do something, please. It's killing me to see you like this."

"How is Jory today?" Malakai asked, changing the subject.

Stavion sighed, and Malakai removed his arm from his face to blink up at his friend. "He's still afraid of me. I don't know what to do. I've tried everything I know, but he all but wets himself every time I step into the room."

"Give him time, Stavion. Does he know you're his mate?"

Stavion shrugged. "I don't know. I've tried explaining it to him, but he won't even look at me. He keeps his eyes closed and trembles whenever I walk into the room."

"Maybe Willow can help," Malakai offered as he struggled to push himself upright. "He talks to Willow, right?"

Stavion nodded, but he didn't look happy about it. "I didn't come here to push my problems on you." He gripped Malakai's shoulder and squeezed. "Are you still going to the wedding?"

"I don't know. If I go, I have to see him with someone else, knowing that he doesn't want me. If I stay, he'll know why, and it makes me look weak."

"So, go and take a date."

Malakai's head snapped up and his eyes widened. "Why would I do that?"

Stavion chuckled. "Malakai, if Boston has another mate, you do realize this man belongs to you as well, right?"

No, he hadn't known that. So, now he had two mates that didn't want him? *Just fucking peachy.* "What does that have to do with me taking someone else to Keeton and Logan's wedding?"

"Show them what they're missing. It's my understanding that

shifters are extremely territorial and possessive. Just think how nuts they'd be if they saw you with another man."

Malakai shook his head firmly. "I don't want to trick them into wanting me."

"That's not possible. If they want you, they'll claim you. If they truly feel nothing for you, well, at least you'll know and have a shoulder to cry on."

"It seems so manipulative."

Stavion beamed and wiggled his eyebrows. "I know."

Rolling his eyes, Malakai chuckled under his breath. "So, who would I take with me? I don't socialize much, Stavion."

"We're all going. Ask one of the guys."

Malakai thought it over quickly. He was friends with all the Enforcers and loved them like brothers. Would it be weird to pretend a relationship with one of them? "Who should I ask?"

"Who says you have to pick just one?"

Oh, Stavion was having way too much fun with this. "I'm not exactly comfortable asking any of them to do this, let alone all of them."

"Fine." Stavion sighed dramatically. "Ask Raven. He's the biggest slut of the bunch, not to mention the biggest instigator. He'll be more than happy to help."

"What if he says no?"

"He won't." Stavion rose from the bed and crossed the room. Peeking over his shoulder, he smiled wickedly. "He's wanted in your pants for years." Then he hurried out the door, leaving Malakai choking and sputtering behind him.

* * * *

"Boston, could I have a minute?"

"Sure." Boston didn't even look up from the book he was reading. Hopefully, if he remained aloof, Flynn would say whatever he needed to say and get the hell out of his room. Every second he spent with the big shifter was just asking for trouble. Even with Flynn still standing in the doorway, Boston could smell his scent, and it made him crazy.

"I'm leavin'," Flynn said after a long pause. "I thought ya should know."

Boston couldn't breathe. His hands trembled, making his book shake, but still he couldn't look at Flynn. "When?"

"I asked Blaise if I could stay until after the weddin'. After that, I'll be reassigned to somewhere I'm bein' needed."

You're needed here, Boston wanted to say. Instead, all he managed was, "Oh." He wouldn't ask Flynn to stay. Maybe it was better this way. So, then why did his heart feel like it was trying to crawl up his throat?

Flynn waited as though he hoped Boston would say more. When he didn't, Flynn sighed. "Will ya even miss me?"

With his heart pounding in his throat, Boston couldn't answer. He didn't know what he'd say even if he could. He just knew he needed Flynn out of his room. The man made him weak, and being weak had broken his heart and jaded him in the first place. Apart from his prejudices against vampires, it was also a big reason he'd pushed Malakai away.

"If ya only say the word, I'll stay," Flynn said quietly. He stepped farther into the room, and Boston began to shake so badly that he dropped his book. "Say it." The end of the bed dipped under his weight as he crawled up the mattress.

Boston pressed back into the headboard, fisted his hands in his lap, and squeezed his eyes closed. Flynn's sweet breath fanned over his face, assaulting his senses, and making his head spin. "Ask me to stay, *a ghrá*. Open your eyes and see me, not just look, but really be seein' me."

He took one of Boston's hands, uncurled his from his tightly clenched fist, and pressed it flat against his chest. "*Mo chroí.*"

My heart. Boston swallowed hard around the burn in his throat. He refused to cry like some lovesick teenage girl mourning the loss of her first crush. Flynn was so much more than a crush, though. He was Boston's mate, his *sienota*, and a piece of himself he'd been missing for too long.

Flynn's lips brushed over his, and every memory, every feeling, came flooding back to him. Stolen kisses, covert looks, whispered endearments—it all assailed him. He remembered it all, the screaming, the pain, the fear, and the gut-wrenching knowledge that each day could be his last.

"Why?" he whispered against Flynn's soft lips. "Why didn't you want me?"

"I did. I do."

Boston pulled away from Flynn's mouth and shook his head as he finally opened his eyes to look at the man. "I saw you. I saw you with him."

Sitting back on his heels, Flynn's eyebrows drew together in confusion. "What did ya see, Boston?"

"You let him fuck you." The words tasted like bile on his tongue. When he'd woken in the middle of the night to the sounds of grunting and moaning, he hadn't thought much of it. But, when he'd seen Flynn's body draped over one of the small tables, his skin shimmering with perspiration in the candlelight, he had crawled over and thrown up right there in his little corner of the basement.

Flynn's face paled, his eyes widened, and he swallowed hard enough to make his Adam's apple bob. "Ya were never meant to see that."

"Never?" How many times had it happened? How many times had Flynn snuck off to be with another man after whispering words of love and forever into Boston's ear?

Flynn swallowed again and licked his lips. "It meant nothin'." The lie was in his eyes and the tight set of his shoulders.

"Even after all these years, you still can't tell me the truth." Boston snorted derisively. "Get out."

"So that be why ya sent me away."

"Get out," Boston repeated icily.

To his surprise and disappointment, Flynn dipped his head, rolled from the bed, and walked to the door. He paused just inside the doorway, his head hung and his fist clenched at his sides. "Everything I have ever done, it was all for you." Then he walked out of the room without a backward glance.

Though Boston wanted to scoff at the statement, something in Flynn's tone made his heart ache. There was sadness in his voice, but something else as well—not guilt, but something like…shame.

"Damn it," Boston growled. Who the hell did the guy think he was just walking away after saying something like that? If he wanted Boston so much, the least he could do was stay and fight for him.

Shoving up from the bed, he marched out of the room and across the hall to bang on Flynn's door. He didn't wait for an answer before barging in and crossing his arms over his chest in a defensive posture. "Would you care to explain what the hell you mean by that?"

"Not particularly, no."

"I think I deserve an explanation."

"That ya do, but…" Flynn trailed off and pushed both hands through his shoulder-length black hair. "Aye, I did it, but I bloody well didn't enjoy it."

"Then why did you do it?"

"It was the only way. Let it be, Boston."

"Not going to happen. I want to know how many times you told me you loved me then waited until I fell asleep to fuck someone else." Boston knew he was being a crass bastard, but he figured he had a right.

"Every time," Flynn whispered, and Boston felt like he'd been punched in the gut.

"Tell me why, Flynn. If you didn't want me for a mate, I can accept that. But why lead me on when you didn't mean it? I was young, but so were you. Was it just some big game to you? Why did you do it?" He yelled the last words, his chest heaving with anger and betrayal.

"To protect you!" Flynn shouted right back. "I let those bloodsuckers have my arse to protect *you*."

Boston's legs began to shake, and he gripped the doorknob to keep from falling to the floor. "Tell me everything."

"That's all there is. I couldn't let them hurt ya that way."

Losing the battle with his legs, Boston sank to the floor and stared up at his mate. "Why didn't you ever tell me?"

Flynn chuckled darkly as he paced the small room. "Do ya think I have no heart, that I would hurt ya like that? I thought I would die the night they took ya away." Flynn stopped and knelt on the floor in front of Boston. "I can't be askin' ya to forgive me."

"How did you get free?" And how much suffering had Flynn endured in Boston's absence?

"I would imagine the same way as you. Drained and tied to a tree."

"Oh, Flynn."

"I came for ya," Flynn whispered, inching closer to Boston. "As soon as I could, I came for ya."

"And I sent you away." Boston closed his eyes and breathed deeply.

"Then the next day ya were gone."

"Well, they kind of burned down our house." Boston tried to defend his actions to make himself feel like less of the asshole he knew he was. His only excuse was that he'd been young, traumatized, and heartbroken. Still, if he'd listened to Flynn that night rather than spouting all the hateful things he'd said, he could have saved them both years of pain. "So, what do we do now?"

"What do ya want? I still be waitin' to hear the words, *a ghrá*."

Boston couldn't stop the smile that spread over his face. "Am I still your love, Flynn?"

"Aye, always. Though, I imagine you're going to have to learn to share." He winked mischievously. "We do have a mate that we'reneedin' to bring home."

Boston flinched and averted his eyes. "I was so cruel to him. I doubt he'll want anything to do with me."

"He'll forgive ya. Ya have to open your heart and be honest with him, though. I'll be right beside ya. Now, say it." Flynn leaned closer and flicked his tongue over Boston's lips. "Say it."

Melting into Flynn's touch, Boston closed his eyes and sighed. "Stay."

Chapter Four

"Is he here then?" Flynn wrapped his arms around Boston's waist and molded himself to his mate's back. Boston still had hang-ups and trust issues, so they'd yet to consummate their new relationship. Flynn knew how to be patient, though. As long as he could hold Boston in his arms and openly show his affection, he wouldn't push...yet.

Boston sighed and sunk back into his embrace, causing Flynn to smile like an idiot. He loved how responsive his mate was to his touch. He could only imagine what it would be like when he finally got the man naked. "It's still daylight, baby. He won't be here until the ceremony."

"Right." Flynn skimmed his nose along the side of Boston's neck. "I forget he's a vampire. It will take some gettin' used to."

"I never forget." And with that statement, Boston's shoulders tensed and his good mood plummeted. "I don't know if I can do this."

Flynn squeezed him tighter. "Do ya think about him?"

"All the time," Boston admitted.

"What do ya feel when ya be thinkin' about him?"

"Horny." Boston chuckled and shook his head. "He's my mate whether I want him to be or not. I can't help but want him, even against my better judgment."

"He is *our* mate." Flynn wasn't sure how he felt about sharing Boston, especially since he'd just gotten him back. If fate had given him a second mate, there must be a reason for it, though. The bond between mates was sacred, and it gave Flynn hope that welcoming another into their life wouldn't be as difficult as he feared.

Besides, Boston was stressed enough for the both of them. "Don't judge him by the actions of others." Flynn knew it was easier said than done. He'd spent years hating the night dwellers and anything to do with their race. "I'm not saying ya have to give him everything, but ya should at least be givin' him a little. Let him earn your trust, *a ghrá.*"

Boston turned and wrapped his arms around Flynn's neck. "When did you get so wise? You're not that much older than me."

"Ah, but I have an old soul, now don't I?" Flynn laughed and tapped the end of Boston's nose with his fingertip. "Someday soon, I'll tell ya all my secrets." Then he kissed his mate with all the emotion he couldn't put into words. "Today is not that day, though."

"And someday soon, I'll tear down my walls and let you in without reservations." Boston smirked and pecked at Flynn's lips. "Today is not that day, though."

The words hurt a little, but Flynn understood. It had been a long time since they'd known each other. It would take time to earn Boston's trust again. Good thing he was up to the challenge. "Aye, I imagine you're right. I want ya somethin' fierce, Boston Mackey, and I intend to have ya. So don't take too long figurin' things out."

"You guys are adorable, but it's *my* wedding." Keeton stepped into the living room and crossed his arms over his chest. "So, knock it off until after the reception."

Boston pulled out of Flynn's arms and gave a deep, sweeping bow. "As you wish, my princess."

Keeton turned his nose up and sniffed. "Much better." Then he wrapped his arms around his stomach and fell into a fit of giggles. When he finally sobered, he sashayed over to Boston and kissed his cheek. "It's good to have you back."

Boston glanced at Flynn and smiled. Flynn thought his heart would jump right out of his chest at the tender look his mate gave him. Turning back to Keeton, Boston bumped the man with his shoulder and chuckled. "It's good to be back."

"Oh, Flynn, Blaise is looking for you. He's out back helping set up the tables." Keeton flounced toward the stairs. "I have to go make myself delicious. Toodles."

Flynn was ashamed to admit that he'd been avoiding the Hunter since his arrival. He enjoyed his job as an Enforcer and was grateful to Elder Winters for securing the position for him, but he'd give it up in a heartbeat if it came between him and Boston. There were plenty of things he could do that would keep him close to his mate. Maybe he could get a job at the club Boston worked at. Then, at least he'd be able to keep an eye on the younger man and dissuade the patrons from playing grab-ass with what belonged to him.

That was another thing he needed to talk to Boston about, but it could wait. It was a day of joy and celebration, not a time for heavy discussions that would most likely leave them both angry and spoiling for a fight.

"Are you going to talk to Blaise or not?" Boston asked, interrupting his thoughts.

"Aye, I suppose I should."

The corners of Boston's eyes tightened and his lips pressed together. Flynn kissed the man's temple and sighed. "I won't take another assignment."

Boston nodded sharply and pulled away from him. "Then go tell him now."

Whoa, okay. Flynn didn't know what to make of the vehemence in Boston's voice. On one hand, it swelled his heart that his mate wanted to ensure that he remained close. Another part of him rankled at the demanding tone. He might only have a couple inches and twenty pounds on Boston, but he was the alpha in their relationship. It would serve Boston well to remember that.

Crossing his arms over his chest, Boston tilted his head up in defiance. Defiance of what, Flynn didn't have a clue, but he recognized the stubborn set of the man's jaw and the way Boston's nostrils flared as though *Flynn* had pissed *him* off. "You're not going to tell him are you?"

Flynn opened his mouth to reply angrily but stopped when he noticed the slight tremble of Boston's shoulders. Sighing to himself, he closed the distance between them and wrapped his arms around Boston. "Do ya not trust me? Did ya think I would leave ya?"

"I don't know if I trust you," Boston confessed. "I want to, but it's been a long time, Flynn. I barely even know you anymore."

"Aye, ya know me, Boston." Flynn took Boston's hand and placed it over his mate's heart, holding it firmly to his chest. "Look from here." He tapped Boston's face near the corner of his eye. "Not here."

* * * *

The wedding was beautiful. Both men wore white tuxedos and held hands before their friends and loved ones under a canopy of flowers and twinkling lights. Malakai felt his throat constrict with emotions at the look of pure love on both Logan's and Keeton's faces. He'd never seen anything more beautiful than the way the mates looked at each other.

Since their binding was not legal in the state of Georgia, there was no reverend in attendance. Keeton had told Malakai that he didn't need a piece of paper to tell him he was married to Logan. God would recognize their union, and that's all that mattered to him. Malakai couldn't agree more.

As alpha of his own pack, Blaise officiated the ceremony. Malakai didn't know much about pack customs, but Stavion had informed him that it was common for an alpha to oversee the joining ceremony of a mated pair, much the same as a coven leader would for a vampire clan.

When it came time for the couple to say their vows, it soon became apparent that they had written their own. Logan cleared his throat and took both of Keeton's hands in his own.

"I promise to defer to your judgment in all matters pertaining to what I should wear and how I should style my hair. I promise not to hog the television remote, always leave enough hot water in the shower for you, and never complain when you spend hours in front of the mirror before we go somewhere."

Logan took a step closer, dipping his head to look into Keeton's eyes. "I promise to never look at another. You will always be the only one for me. I'll never betray you, never lie to you, and never break your trust. I'll spend every day of my life loving you for the treasure you are. I pledge myself to you." He slipped the small golden band on Keeton's finger. "Always."

Malakai swallowed around the burn in his throat, damning himself for being an oversensitive fool. Looking around at the people gathered there, he noticed he wasn't the only one trying to hold back his emotions. Even the big alpha, Xander, looked a little misty-eyed.

Keeton sniffled and coughed a little before reaching into his pocket and removing a similar ring, though much larger. He took his mate's hands and looked up at him, love and devotion written all over his face.

"I promise not to complain when you leave your dirty socks all over the house, not kick you out of bed when you snore, and never break your nose again."

Malakai startled a little at this, but calmed instantly when chuckles swept through the crowd. Smiling, he promised himself he'd ask Keeton about that after the ceremony.

"I promise to keep the freezer stocked with your favorite ice cream, and not throw the bowl at you when you forget to save me some."

Again the guests laughed. Malakai joined with them, though he didn't have a clue what the man was talking about. He did gather that Logan had his hands full with the feisty little blond.

Keeton took a deep breath and let it out slowly. "I promise to be yours forever. There will never be another for me. I will always wait up for you to come home, always worry for you and take care of you.

I promise to love you every day that you'll let me until we're too old to do more than hold hands on the front porch." He slid the ring onto Logan's finger and smiled, though it looked a little wobbly. "I pledge myself to you always."

In the next breath, Logan had his mate up in his arms, kissing him with enough heat to set the place on fire.

"Hey, break it up!" Blaise shouted, pushing at the pair. Malakai slapped a hand over his mouth to muffle his laughter when Logan broke away from Keeton's mouth, only to snarl at the alpha. Blaise just smirked. "I'm not done yet."

"Make it quick," Logan demanded.

Blaise began speaking, his words sounding official, but from the smile on his face, Malakai had a feeling that he was dragging it out purposely. When he'd finished, he dipped his head and chuckled at Logan's snarl. "I now pronounce you husband and husband. You may—"

That's as far as he got before Logan was attacking Keeton's mouth again. Blaise threw his hands up and huffed. "Why am I even here?"

Laughter and applause rang out through the night. It was the strangest wedding he'd ever attended, but it felt right, and Malakai was happy that he'd been asked to be a part of it.

"Boston's mate is hot," Raven whispered in his ear.

Like letting the helium out of a balloon, Malakai's mood deflated and his stomach knotted. "He is. Thanks for pointing that out." Raven had to be the most tactless person he'd ever met in his life. He knew the big Enforcer hadn't said the words to hurt him, so he bit back his anger.

"I was talking about you, dipshit." Raven leaned back in his chair and chuckled. "You look good in black."

"I'm not sleeping with you," Malakai blurted then covered his face with his hands as his cheeks heated.

Raven just laughed harder. "I didn't think you would." They were silent for a few minutes as the rest of the guests cheered.

Logan and Keeton made their way up the aisle, grinning and waving at everyone. Malakai waved back, though his heart wasn't really in it anymore. This was a stupid idea. He shouldn't have come.

"I think you should kiss me, though," Raven said suddenly.

"What?" Malakai jerked around to stare at the vampire. "Are you crazy?"

"I think you should do it now." Raven wrapped his fingers around the back of Malakai's neck, jerking him forward and crushing their mouths together.

Malakai struggled against the hold, pushing with all his strength against Raven's chest. Fuck, this had been a really, really bad idea.

"Stop being an idiot," Raven growled against his lips. "Boston is coming this way. Kiss me back or fight harder. Either is bound to piss him off, whether it brings out his possessiveness or his protectiveness." Then he mashed his mouth to Malakai's again.

Malakai struggled harder—not because he wanted Boston to feel the need to protect him, but because he felt sick at the thought of being in such an intimate position with someone other than his mate. Even if Boston didn't want him, he still felt like he was being unfaithful. God, he was seriously screwed up.

Boston had a new mate. They probably fucked like rabbits every chance they got. Malakai hadn't even breathed in anyone's direction since the night he'd met the big shifter. Stavion continued to assure him that Boston's mate, Flynn, would also be Malakai's mate. He had serious doubts, though.

Shoving as hard as he could at Raven's shoulders, he wrenched his mouth away and glared. "Stop!"

Raven grinned wickedly and pulled Malakai back to his mouth. An ear-piercing roar ripped through the night, and the next thing Malakai knew, he was jerked out of his seat and wrapped in powerful arms. "Mine!"

To his complete shock and bewilderment, it wasn't Boston, but

Flynn that held him, snarling at Raven like a wild animal. "Mine!" the man repeated with enough savageness to make Malakai shudder.

"Says who?" Raven stood, crossed his arms over his chest, and smirked. He opened his mouth to say something else but was cut off when Boston tackled him to the ground and wound his fingers around Raven's throat.

"I said," Boston growled. "Now, fuck off." He squeezed a little harder before releasing the Enforcer and jumping to his feet to hurry over to Flynn and Malakai.

Malakai didn't even know what to say. People were huddled around, staring at them. Some looked afraid, some shocked, and others were smirking. Flynn nuzzled his nose against the side of Malakai's neck, humming softly.

Boston's hands began roaming over Malakai's cheeks and down his neck. "Are you okay? Did he hurt you?"

Malakai shook his head mutely. His body burned from the touch of his mates. And oh, yes, Stavion was right. Flynn was most definitely his mate as much as Boston. Still, he was confused, and a little leery of Boston's sudden concern for him. What the hell was going on anyway?

A loud rumble vibrated Flynn's chest, and he snapped his head up. "Mine," he snarled again when Raven climbed to his feet and took a step toward them.

Malakai rolled his eyes. The shifter was beginning to sound like a broken record. "I'm fine, but I'm not sure that I'm *yours.*"

"Of course ya are." Flynn sounded so matter-of-fact, as though it was the simplest thing in the world. Malakai whimpered a little at the man's sexy brogue. "Ya belong to me."

"And me," Boston added quietly. "I was an idiot."

Malakai wasn't sure about the past tense of that statement. As far as he was concerned, Boston was still an idiot. "Put me down."

"No."

"No?" Malakai glared up at Flynn. Who the hell did he think he was anyway?

Boston chuckled. "You'll get used to it."

"I won't be sticking around long enough to get used to anything," Malakai shot back. "You don't want me." He jerked his thumb up toward Flynn. "And he's just crazy."

"He smells good," Flynn crooned, nuzzling into Malakai's hair, completely oblivious to Malakai's last statement. "He's just a wee thing, isn't he? I like how he fits in my arms."

"*He* has a name, and I'm right here."

"And fierce, I see." Flynn chuckled softly, his warm breath stuttering over the sensitive flesh on Malakai's neck.

Boston frowned. "He was really proper when I met him, kind of stuffy."

Malakai bristled. They were still talking about him like he wasn't there, and now Boston was insulting him. Well, there wasn't any part of him that was feeling *proper* at the moment. Growling loudly, he felt his fangs burst through his gums and bared his teeth.

The blood drained from Boston's face, his body began to shake, and he stumbled backward so fast that he tripped over a chair and fell on his ass, banging the back of his head off the seat on his descent.

"Oh, no." Malakai slapped his hand over his mouth, wincing when his sharp canines poked his lip. He never lost control like that. He never got angry. Guilt swarmed him as he renewed his struggle against Flynn's hold. "Please. I'm sorry. Just let me go!"

"Jesus, Malakai, be still!" Flynn tightened his arms and huffed. "I'll put ya on your feet, but ya are not to move. Am I clear?"

Sighing in resignation, Malakai stopped fighting and dipped his head. "As crystal." It wasn't as if he had anywhere to go, and he didn't think the night could possibly get any worse.

And that's what he got for thinking.

Chapter Five

His stomach rolled violently. Boston gritted his teeth to keep from tossing his cookies all over the grass. Sweat poured off him in rivers, and he damned himself for being weak and making a jackass out of himself.

"Boston?"

He heard a voice whisper his name, but he couldn't focus.

"Boston?"

Blinking up stupidly, the world came rushing back to Boston, and he found Malakai kneeling next to him on the ground. The close proximity of the vampire sent Boston into a panic once again, and he scrambled backward away from the man. The back of his head connected with the metal chair, causing him to hiss in pain. "Stop!"

Malakai held his hands up in surrender and eased away from him. "I'm sorry, Boston. I didn't mean to lose my temper. I won't hurt you."

Boston felt like a complete idiot. This tiny vampire was trying to comfort him. He doubted Malakai even reached the middle of his chest, but Boston was terrified of him. While he'd fought vehemently against them in that diner, he'd been prepared—recognizing them for what they were the minute they stepped up to their table. That didn't mean that he hadn't been scared out of his mind, but at least he'd had a little warning.

He hadn't even thought twice about tackling Raven to the ground. A cold, all-consuming rage had come over him when he'd seen his mate in the arms of another man. When it became obvious that Malakai wasn't a willing participant in the tonsil hockey match, he'd wanted to rip the big Enforcer apart, piece by piece.

When Malakai snarled at him and bared his fangs, Boston thought he'd wet himself. He hadn't been prepared for it. One minute, he was stroking Malakai's face, and the next he was on the ground.He'd let his guard down and ended up with a face full of angry vampire.

Every old memory, every pain—every horrible thing he suffered in that basement in Montana—all came rushing back to him, hitting him like a ton of bricks. Why did Malakai affect him so strongly?

Staring up at the smaller man, Boston immediately knew the answer. He couldn't fight back against Malakai. The man could drain him dry, and Boston wouldn't even raise a finger to stop him. It was so strongly ingrained in him to protect his mate that he knew he'd never do anything to hurt Malakai.

"I'm sorry," Malakai apologized again in a strangled whisper. "I should go."

"No," a deep, sexy voice responded. "He'll be fine when he gets his wits about him." Flynn crouched beside Boston and held out his hand. "Aye, Boston?"

Nodding dazedly, Boston took Flynn's hand and allowed the man to help him to his feet. He didn't have a clue what to say to Malakai. His mind and body were a whirlwind of conflicting emotions. His heart still hammered inside his chest, and his legs trembled slightly. On the other hand, his skin tingled, his gums itched, and his stomach fluttered when he looked at the sexy little vampire. His shifter wanted their mate—both of their mates. The human side of Boston was having a little trouble catching up, though.

"Now, let us have a dance, and be gettin' to know one another." Flynn sounded so calm and cool that Boston couldn't help but envy the Irishman.

Letting Flynn lead him out to the makeshift dance floor, Boston tried to ignore the stares they were receiving. Once they stepped onto the slightly raised, wood platform, Flynn pulled Malakai in between them and wound his arms around the man's waist. Looking over

Malakai's head, he met Boston's eyes and gave a curt dip of his head.

Taking a deep breath, Boston reached out tentatively, and rested his hands on Malakai's hips, just above Flynn's arms. He immediately jerked them away and hissed. His fingers tingled like he'd been zapped with electricity. The current traveled to his gut then made a beeline for his groin, causing his dick to swell in record time.

He'd become accustomed to beating back his body's reaction to Flynn. Malakai was new, though, and something about being in the presence of both his mates set Boston's body on fire. Watching Malakai flinch and step closer to Flynn made him feel about two inches tall.

Swallowing hard and trying to tame his lust, Boston rested his hands on Malakai's hips once more, and groaned when his body lit up again. He kept a distance between their bodies, not wanting Malakai to feel the erection tenting the front of his slacks. No matter how much he wanted the little vampire, he knew he still had issues to work through, and it wouldn't be fair to tease Malakai like that.

No one spoke as they swayed gently to the music. Boston raked his eyes over Malakai's back, taking in his slim shoulders, lean waist, and perfectly shaped ass. His conservative haircut fit him perfectly, and the silky strands gleamed in the soft, twinkling lights.

A soft groan reached his ears, making his cock throb painfully, and Boston realized it had come from Malakai. Coming out of his daze, he also realized that while he'd been drinking in the sight of Malakai's backside, his hands had been caressing the vampire's hips and up his sides.

Boston started to panic, but a sweet whimper fell from Malakai's lips, and all he could think about was getting inside his mate's tight ass. Taking a chance, willing himself not to freak out, he shuffled closer to Malakai until his chest pressed against the man's back.

Closing his eyes, Boston almost passed out from the pleasure that the simple act brought him. Malakai was so warm, his scent much stronger so close, and Boston couldn't deny his desire to feel the man's body with no barriers between them.

"What did I tell ya?" Flynn chuckled and placed a chaste kiss on the top of Malakai's head. "I be tellin' ya he'd come around soon enough."

Boston's eyes snapped open, but he couldn't bring himself to release his hold on Malakai or step away from him. He loved the contact too much, and his stag was ready to gore him in the balls if he didn't do something to keep their mate with them.

"Yes," he rasped hoarsely. "I'm fine, Malakai."

"I'm so sorry, Boston. I didn't mean to frighten you." Malakai tried to turn, but Boston held him tight to prevent it.

Very slowly, he bent forward and brushed his lips over the side of Malakai's neck. The shiver he received in response made him feel like a god. "I'm fine." He skimmed his nose along Malakai's throat, loving the smell of the man. "I want you to stay, Malakai. Give me a chance to explain and make things right. I can't promise that I won't freak out again, but I want to try."

"Boston, I'm not sure that's a good idea."

"Aye, it be a fine idea." Flynn nipped Malakai's earlobe in reprimand, and even Boston trembled from the act. "Ya be doin' what I tell ya now, Malakai. We be takin' care of ya."

Boston stood tall, cocked his head to the side, and frowned. Flynn was laying the Irish brogue on pretty damn thick. The man didn't talk like that, so what the hell was going on?

Flynn met his eyes and winked before nodding down at Malakai. Boston still didn't have a clue what the man was up to.

"Flynn," Malakai began. "Your name is Flynn, right?"

"Aye, but I think ya can be callin' me whatever ya like, and I not be getting' upset."

That's when Boston saw it. Every word that poured from Flynn's mouth in that thick accent and dialect sent a shudder through Malakai's body until the man was barely standing on his own feet. "Oh, you are wrong, Flynn Murphy."

Flynn smiled at him innocently. "Just usin' the gifts God be givin' me."

Boston snorted and rolled his eyes. "You're an idiot."

"You're both idiots," Malakai said with a snort of his own. "I'm not staying here."

"Of course ya are," Flynn replied immediately, dropping the heavy brogue. The accent was still there, though, and sexy as sin. Boston could definitely understand Malakai's reaction to Flynn's voice as the vampire shivered again.

Malakai shook his head and took a step to the side away from them. "Look, he doesn't want me." He pointed to Boston. "I barely even know you," he continued, turning his attention back to Flynn. "You two obviously know each other, and have something special together. I don't want to get in the way of that."

"I want ya," Flynn answered, stepping closer to Malakai.

Boston did, too, but he couldn't make his mouth work to say the words.

Malakai looked sad. "I want you, too, Flynn. I can't be happy with just one mate when I know I have two, though. I don't mind sharing mutually, but I'm not okay with you hopping from my bed to Boston's. I need to go."

"No," Boston growled. He still didn't know what his feelings for Malakai were, but the man was his mate, and vampire or not, he wanted Malakai with him—with them. "Just give me some time. I do want you, Malakai, but there's a lot you don't know."

"Then tell me."

"I will, but not here." Boston scanned the crowd gathered on their back lawn. "Will you stay? Give me…a week. One week, and if you're still not happy, I'll personally see to it that you get home safely."

Malakai chewed his bottom lip and his eyebrows scrunched together as he thought it over. "That seems reasonable," he finally said. "I can't be in the sunlight, though. I'll need a place to sleep during the day where I won't fry." He turned and tilted his head up to Flynn. "What do you think about this?"

"I want ya with us." Flynn crossed his arms over his chest and glared as if the entire conversation was offending him. "This is where ya belong, Malakai..." He trailed off and cocked and eyebrow. "I'm not knowin' ya last name."

"Bruins. My name is Malakai Bruins."

"Well then, Malakai Bruins, it be a pleasure to finally meet ya."

Malakai's attention snapped to Boston. "You told him about me?"

Boston blushed, but dipped his head in affirmation. "I did. I'm sorry I was such a dick. Maybe after I tell you my story, you'll understand, and maybe be able to forgive me after a while."

To his intense relief, Malakai's eyes softened, and he held his hand out to Boston. "I think I'd like that."

With only a slight hesitation, Boston reached out and took Malakai's hand, sighing when their skin met. He had been a fool to think he could live without this. Just being with his men gave him such a deep sense of peace and belonging. He was finally beginning to understand all the hoopla about *sienotas*. He finally felt...complete.

"I need to talk to Stavion."

"I'll come with you," Boston whispered. Wherever his mates went was where he wanted to be.

"Aye, as will I." The tone of Flynn's voice was totally possessive.

Malakai rolled his eyes, but Boston just smiled and tugged Malakai close to him. "Don't be too hard on him. I'm not the only one with a story to tell."

"I understand," Malakai whispered. "Let's find my coven leader and make the arrangements for my stay."

Boston's grin stretched wider, and he tapped the end of Malakai's nose. "I like how you talk."

To his delight, Malakai flushed a soft pink and ducked his head. "I know I can be a bit formal sometimes."

Slipping his fingers under his mate's chin, Boston urged

Malakai's face up toward his. Steeling his courage, he bent forward, pausing before their lips touched—partly to gauge his comfort level, and partly to seek permission.

Malakai's eyes widened and his tongue darted out to moisten his lips. Boston groaned at the sight, closed the distance between them, and pressed their mouths together softly. Oh, God, he was so screwed. Kissing Malakai was like sticking his tongue to a battery, and he didn't think he'd ever get enough.

Pulling away, he stared into Malakai's soft amber eyes, completely hypnotized. "Don't apologize. I wasn't teasing you. I do like how you talk."

"Thank you."

Straightening, Boston took Malakai's hand and turned to Flynn, desperately seeking the man's approval. He really didn't have any clue what he was doing, but he knew Flynn wouldn't let him fall.

Flynn smiled crookedly, wrapped his fingers around the back of Boston's neck, and pulled him into a tender kiss. "It's a good start, *a ghrá*. I'm proud of ya, I am." Then he kissed Boston again, flicking his tongue over his lips and seeking entrance.

Boston opened with a happy sigh, groaning softly at the first brush of Flynn's tongue against his own. Malakai's needy whimper had him pulling away from Flynn and chuckling. "I think someone needs a little attention."

Winking, Flynn pulled Malakai up in his arms, spun him around, and planted a searing kiss on his mouth. Boston laughed like a loon at the look on Malakai's face. The little vamp might as well get used to it. That's just how Flynn Murphy was. Boston adored the Irishman's love of life.

"Do ya think ya have been sufficiently loved on now, my darlin'?"

Malakai's eyes were wide and dazed, and he nodded silently. Boston pressed his lips together to keep from laughing again. He took Malakai's hand when Flynn set him on his feet and gave a little tug.

"Let's go find the boss man."

Seeing the sweet smile on Malakai's face and the wicked grin on Flynn's, Boston knew he was making the right decision.

I can do this.

Chapter Six

Sweet hell, was he seriously considering this?

Malakai rubbed at his face with his free hand as he allowed Boston to lead him through the throng of people in their search for Stavion. What was his best friend going to say? Would he be angry that Malakai had given in so easily? Would he be happy for him that things might actually work out with his mates?

Why the hell did it even matter what anyone else thought? All Malakai had ever wanted was to be loved and accepted. He had that with Stavion and the other Enforcers, of course, but it wasn't exactly the same. They were always there for him, but they didn't bring light to his endlessly dark existence.

"What are you thinking so hard about?" Boston asked, interrupting his thoughts. "It's going to be fine, baby. I promise."

Malakai felt the dopey grin stretch over his face at the endearment. He doubted Boston even realized he'd said it. Malakai certainly wasn't going to inform him. Damn, Boston and Flynn smelled like heaven. He could just imagine how sweet their blood tasted.

The thought pulled him up short, and he came to an abrupt halt, jerking Boston to a stop as well. Considering the way Boston flipped out from the sight of Malakai's fangs, he seriously doubted his mate would be open to feeding him. He wasn't sure how Flynn felt about it, and he was a little afraid to broach the subject. It was important, though. He couldn't survive without blood.

"What's wrong?" Boston caressed Malakai's cheek with his knuckles, staring at his hand as though he couldn't believe what he was doing. "I thought you needed to talk to Stavion?"

"I do." Sucking his bottom lip between his teeth, Malakai tried to find the words. "I have to feed," he ended up blurting. There just wasn't an easy way to tell someone that you wanted to make a snack out of their neck.

Flynn stepped up beside Boston and frowned. "Right now?"

"No, but soon." He didn't want to say anything, but it would need to be damn soon. He'd been taking less and less from the donors at the coven. Ever since he'd met Boston and had known his mate was out there, it turned his stomach to drink from someone else. It felt like a betrayal, which was completely stupid considering that Boston hadn't wanted him. Still, he couldn't help how he felt.

Boston's brow wrinkled, and he looked to be thinking very hard. "Can you stay here with Flynn for a minute? I'll be right back."

Panic flared in Malakai's heart, and he squeezed Boston's hand tighter. Was the man going to run again? He didn't know if he'd survive it a second time.

His mate smiled softly and bent to kiss Malakai's forehead. "I promise I'll be right back." Before he could walk away, though, the man they'd been searching for found them.

"Malakai," Stavion called with a radiant smile.

"Never mind," Boston mumbled under his breath.

Malakai didn't know what to make of that, so he ignored it and greeted his best friend with a hug. Rolling his eyes at the soft growls from behind him, he released Stavion and quickly introduced his mates. "You know Boston of course, and this is Flynn Murphy."

The three offered their greetings with stiff nods of their heads as they sized each other up. Malakai just sighed. He'd never understand alpha males if he lived forever. All the growling and snarling was completely immature as far as he was concerned.

"So, I guess you'll be staying in Georgia," Stavion finally said after a long, strained silence. His eyes never left Boston as he spoke. "Are you sure that's a good idea?"

"Honestly, no." Malakai squeezed Boston's hand again when his mate's head snapped around to look at him in shock. "It's what I need to do, though. I owe Boston a chance, and Flynn has done nothing to me."

"Should I send your stuff?" Stavion asked, finally settling his gaze on Malakai.

"Not yet. We've decided to give it a week. If I'm not at least on my way to being happy, I'm free to come home."

"I don't like this."

"You don't have to." He released Boston's hand and crossed his arms over his thin chest. "I would like your support, but I don't need it."

Stavion looked like he'd been slapped in the face. After another awkward silence, he rubbed his hand over his jaw and groaned. "You're right. I'm sorry. I just worry about you. When's the last time you've had blood?"

Malakai echoed Stavion's groan and closed his eyes. "I'm fine for a while longer."

"You're lying. Did you feed at all before we left?"

"Stavion, drop it. I said I'm fine."

"Then tell me when's the last time you fed!" Stavion growled and his hand came up.

Malakai had no idea what the man intended to do with that hand, and he didn't get a chance to find out. Flynn and Boston tackled Stavion to the ground, snarling at him like a couple of rabid dogs. *God save me from fools.*

Rushing over, he pulled on Boston's shoulder, trying to get his mate's attention. "Boston, let him up. He wasn't going to hurt me."

Boston looked up at him and shook his head a few times. "What?" His attention snapped back to Stavion, then to Flynn. "Oh," he breathed. Slowly, he climbed off of Stavion and urged Flynn to do the same.

Stavion rose to his feet and casually brushed the grass from his suit as though nothing had happened. "I was just frustrated. I wasn't going to hit him," he said quietly.

"Sorry, man," Boston mumbled in obvious embarrassment.

While decidedly violent, his mates' actions went a long way in convincing Malakai that he should stay and try to make this relationship work. It was the second time in less than an hour that his men had come to his rescue. Not that he'd needed it either time, but the sentiment was appreciated nonetheless.

Stavion waved away the apology. "I'm feeling pretty damn good right now. After what happened in Wyoming, I'm not your biggest fan when it comes to Malakai." He looked at Boston in a calculating manner. "You're willingness to protect him makes me feel better about leaving him here, though."

"You idiots really need to stop talking about me like I'm not here." Malakai's happy mood was on a downward spiral from hell. "I might be small, but I'm perfectly capable of taking care of myself. I don't need a babysitter, a keeper, or a bodyguard."

"Now, Malakai," Flynn started to say, but Malakai held his hand up to cut the man off.

"I am an adult, not to mention a vampire. I appreciate everyone's concern, but I'm not a child or a new toy for you three to fight over."

Stavion nodded curtly. Boston sighed and scrubbed at his face. Flynn just smirked. *Yeah, well fuck them all.* Straightening his tie, Malakai smoothed down the lapels of his jacket and stuck his nose in the air. "I'm going to congratulate the happy couple. I expect everyone to at least be civil by the time I return." He strode off without another word, snickering quietly to himself at the stunned look on the men's faces.

Footsteps sounded behind him, and a warm hand wrapped around his own. "I'm sorry," Boston whispered. "I didn't mean to treat you like a child or like your wants and opinions aren't important. This mating thing is new to me. When I thought he was going to hurt you, my instincts took over. I know you don't need me."

Oh, how wrong you are, Boston Mackey. Instead of saying anything, Malakai just squeezed his mate's hand and smiled.

"I was sold by my pack when I was sixteen," Boston said so quietly that Malakai almost didn't hear him. "For three years I was kept in a basement and used as a blood slave by a vampire coven in Montana. That's where I met Flynn."

Malakai didn't even realize he'd stopped walking until Boston turned to stand in front of him. He had no idea what to say. His poor mate must have lived through hell. He'd heard stories, seen firsthand the destruction being held prisoner could do to one's psyche. "How do I help?"

Boston reached out and cupped his cheek, brushing away a stray tear with the pad of his thumb. "Don't cry, baby. It was a long time ago. I just want you to know why this is so hard for me. I'm trying, though."

His mate was alpha to the core, so Malakai could only imagine how much it hurt the man's pride to confess such things to him. He didn't want to make things harder for Boston. "We'll go slow. Just let me know if I do something to make you uncomfortable."

"I really like you, Malakai, and I want to make this work. Don't give up on me, okay?"

Malakai smiled and nodded. He tried to start walking again, but Boston held him in place with his large hands on Malakai's shoulders. "I know you need to feed. I'm not sure I'm up for that yet, but I'm not going to let you starve. I don't know how Flynn feels, but his story might just be worse than mine."

There was so much sadness in Boston's voice, Malakai wanted to wrap the big shifter in his arms and make it all disappear. Unsure if the act would be welcomed, he did nothing. This was going to be a lot harder than he'd originally assumed. He thought Boston just had some prejudice against vampires. Turns out, he did, but with good reason. Would he ever be able to escape his past and trust Malakai?

"We'll figure something out, though, okay? Just...don't leave, okay?"

The sadness bled out until Boston just sounded lost. Malakai's heart was breaking, and he was trying so hard to hold his emotions in check. "I'm not going anywhere." Where would he go? As long as his mates were willing to try, he was exactly where he needed to be. Maybe in time he'd find a way to heal Boston's broken spirit. "Let's find Logan and Keeton."

"They already disappeared." Boston chuckled a little. "I think Logan was a little…excited."

"Then maybe we should start finding me a place to sleep. A closet will do in a pinch, but it's not the most comfortable place in the world."

Boston frowned. "Does the room need to be pitch-black during the day?"

"No. Since I'm part shifter, it's not quite as bad for me as it is for the others. I still can't go out in the day, not even when it's cloudy. A little light in the room is okay, as long as it's not shining directly on me."

"Flynn," Boston called. He waited for the man to trot up next to them and motioned toward Malakai. "We need to find a place for Malakai to sleep, and then I think we need to talk."

"Well, then let's get to it." Flynn bent and pecked at Malakai's lips before standing straight and grinning. "Will ya be needin' anything else, then?"

"He needs to feed," Boston answered before Malakai could answer in the negative. "I can't do it." He sounded ashamed, but again, Malakai didn't know how to help him.

"Aye, that's a problem all right. Would ya be opposed to drinkin' from the wrist?"

Malakai shook his head quickly. It wasn't nearly as intimate as he wanted to be with his mates, but understanding their background with vampires, he was willing to compromise.

"Then we'll not worry." That's all he said before grabbing them both by the wrists and practically dragging them toward the house. "Say farewell to everyone as we pass because we'll not be stoppin'."

Malakai looked quickly to Boston as he hurried to keep up with Flynn's long strides. He burst into laughter at the confused look on the man's face. Apparently, Boston had no more clue what Flynn was up to than he did.

Flynn pulled them along until they'd reached a dark, secluded section near the side of the house. Without warning or preliminaries, he lifted Malakai into his arms and crushed their mouths together. Urging Malakai to wrap around him like second skin, he walked them forward until Malakai's back pressed against the side of the house.

Licking, biting, and sucking, Flynn ravished him. Malakai couldn't catch his breath, and he wasn't sure he wanted to. Sweet mercy, Flynn tasted amazing. The kiss was feral, almost savage in its intensity. No one had ever handled him in such a way. Because of his smaller size, his bed partners were always gentle, tender, and it drove Malakai up the fucking wall.

Jerking away long seconds later, Flynn dropped his forehead to Malakai's shoulder and panted for breath. Malakai was doing quite a bit of huffing and puffing himself, but before his head had even stopped spinning, Boston was there. Strong fingers gripped his chin, while Boston's other hand fisted in his hair. Then Malakai was ravished all over again.

The possessive growl that rumbled in Boston's chest was like music to his ears. Keeping a firm hold on Flynn, Malakai wrapped his other arm around Boston's neck to hold him in place as their tongues dueled. The impressive bulge behind Flynn's zipper rubbed against the hard cock trapped inside Malakai's slacks.

His dick throbbed and strained, screaming for freedom. Continuing his assault on Boston's mouth, Malakai rocked against Flynn, seeking the much needed friction that he craved. God, he was so close already, and he still had all of his clothes on. It was the second time that night that he felt himself losing control, but this time he craved the loss.

Flynn's hands roamed his body, pulling his shirttail free of his slacks and gliding his callused hands over Malakai's taut abs while his lips trailed down the side of his neck. Malakai hissed into Boston's mouth, loving the feel of his mates' hands and lips on him. His balls churned and ached, his dick pulsed, and the need to come overwhelmed him.

Lost in the mind-numbing pleasure his men were giving him, Malakai shut down his brain and let his body take over—which was completely fucking stupid. The minute he let go of his rigid control, his fangs shot through his gums and pierced Boston's lower lip. His mate gasped, jerked away, and stumbled backward several unsteady steps.

Licking the blood off his canine, Malakai couldn't stop his groan. He'd been right. Boston was the sweetest thing he'd ever tasted in his life. It had been so long since he'd had blood in any quantity, and his body began to tremble with need.

It took about three seconds for his brain to catch up with the rest of him, and when it did, Malakai wanted to scream, or cry, or hit something. His mate had trusted him, and he'd messed up royally. Looking first up at Flynn, then to Boston, Malakai closed his eyes and dropped his head back to the wall behind him. "I'm so sorry. I can't help my body's reaction to you, but that's no excuse. I should have warned you or made you back off. I should have done something, but I'm selfish, and I didn't want you to stop touching me."

His babbling apology was cut short by Boston's tongue down his throat. He knew it was Boston, not only by scent, but by the almost desperate way he licked at the inside of Malakai's mouth. It felt as though the man was trying to prove to himself that he could do this— that he could still desire Malakai, fangs and all.

"Stop," he panted, pushing at Boston's chest. "You don't have to do this."

"Shut up," Boston snarled before attacking his mouth again.

"No!" He pushed hard at Boston and struggled to free himself from Flynn's hold. "Stop, please," he begged. When Flynn sat him on his feet, and he finally had their attention, he ran a hand through his hair and breathed deeply to calm himself. "Stavion was right. I haven't fed in almost a week, and I never take much when I do—not nearly enough. I'm barely holding on to my control right now. I don't want to do anything to scare you, so we need to stop."

"Why haven't you taken what you needed?" Boston asked quietly, taking a step closer.

Malakai held his hands up to ward off the shifter's advance while he tried to come up with something that wasn't an absolute lie. He couldn't very well tell Boston the truth, though. He hadn't brought it up to make his mate feel guilty, but to explain why they needed to slow things down.

"Malakai?" Flynn asked in that voice that turned Malakai's legs to Jell-O.

"It...I..." Damn it, what did he tell them?

"Tell me the truth," Boston demanded.

Oh, well that sounded just dandy in theory. The confusion and concern in his mates' eyes finally wore him down, though. "After I returned to my coven, I had a hard time drinking from the donors. It felt wrong and made my stomach cramp."

"Was there something wrong with the donors?" Boston asked in confusion.

Flynn looked at Malakai with more understanding than he wanted to see. The Irishman knew exactly why Malakai hadn't wanted to drink from those men and women.

Fidgeting under Flynn's scrutiny, he debated on how to explain it to Boston.

"Aye, something was very wrong," Flynn said before Malakai could work through his jumbled thoughts.

"What? What happened?" Boston gripped Flynn's shoulders and shook him a little. "I'm freaking the fuck out here. Will you please just tell me what's going on?"

Cradling Boston's face in both palms, Flynn kissed him slow and sweet. Malakai's chest constricted with emotion, even while his dick went hard once more. Less than noble images of the two big men, naked, sweaty, and writhing together slipped through his mind. Malakai could only hope he'd be around long enough to live the fantasy one day.

"They weren't my mates," Malakai whispered when the pair came up for oxygen. He wasn't a coward. While he appreciated Flynn's help, it wasn't the man's responsibility. "I hated drinking from them because I felt like I was being disloyal to you."

Boston winced. "Even though I treated you like shit?"

"You didn't treat me badly. You just didn't want me. I still can't help how I felt."

Unsurprisingly, Boston spun on his heels and stomped around the side of the house without a word. Flynn sighed and fisted his hand in his long, raven hair. It was on the tip of Malakai's tongue to apologize, but before he could get the words out through his clogged throat, Flynn sighed again and held his hand out. "I'm thinkin' he's more upset with himself than with you. Come on now."

Putting his trust in Flynn, Malakai took the man's hand and just prayed he hadn't made the biggest mistake of his life.

Chapter Seven

"Where are we going?"

"To find Xander."

"Wait. I thought we were going to talk to Boston."

Flynn sighed but kept walking. "I think we're needin' to start at the beginin'." Well, that wasn't strictly true. The beginning started well before he'd ever met Boston in that dank basement. Still, he hoped Xander would have a little insight of how to get through to their confused mate. It hurt that he didn't know Boston well enough anymore to help him, but he wasn't too proud to call in reinforcements.

Malakai was silent as they made their way through the partygoers and out onto the dance floor. They found Xander wrapped around Braxton, swaying his little mate to the music and smiling that special smile that only those in love could wear. Flynn hated to interrupt them, but his questions couldn't wait.

"Xander?"

"Hey, Flynn Malakai." Xander dipped his head in greeting, not releasing Braxton. "Where's Boston?"

"Could we talk to you?" Malakai asked.

Xander's eyebrows drew together, but he nodded and stepped back from Braxton. "Sure, what's going on?"

"I'm needin' some information on Boston," Flynn replied quietly. "He's hurtin'."

"C'mon," Braxton said just as softly. "Let's grab one of the empty tables, and we'll talk." Pulling his mate off the dance floor, he led them to a table and motioned for everyone to take a seat. "I don't know much about Boston, but I want to help if I can."

Flynn nodded his appreciation. It warmed his heart that even though he hadn't been there for his mate, Boston had people who cared about him and wanted to see him happy. Giving a brief overview of the events that unfolded around the side of the house, Flynn only divulged as much as he thought necessary. Malakai was already blushing, and he didn't want to embarrass the little man if he could help it.

"Then he just left," Malakai added when Flynn had finished. "I don't know what to do. Maybe I should just leave."

Flynn's heart broke at the dejected quality of Malakai's voice. Leaning closer, he pressed his lips to the vampire's temple and sighed. "Ya not goin' anywhere."

"He's right," Xander said with a kind smile. "Just give him some time. I don't know all the details of what happened at that coven in Montana. Boston refuses to talk about it." He went on to tell them how they'd found Boston naked, nearly drained, and tied to a tree in the dead of winter with several inches of snow on the ground. "I honestly didn't think he'd make it through the night."

"I don't say this to hurt you." Braxton paused and looked up at Xander. His mate gave him a short nod, which appeared to be what Braxton had been looking for, because he turned back to them and continued. "I've only known Boston for about a year. He doesn't ever bring anyone home. He talks about dating, getting laid, and all that, but I think he's lying."

"How do ya mean?" Flynn gritted his teeth against the jealousy. He wasn't some blushing virgin by any means, but the mention of Boston with another man made his stomach roll. Boston was *his*!

"He's funny, charming, and sweet as pie," Braxton offered. "He's sarcastic and the life of the party. Sometimes when he doesn't think anyone's looking, though, I can see the sadness in his eyes. I think he works really hard to make everyone think he's okay. So, spouting off about an active social life fits right in with that happy-go-lucky lifestyle."

"I don't understand." Malakai rested his elbows on the table and leaned forward. "How does that make you think he's lying?"

"I've lived with the guy for going on nine years now," Xander said slowly. "In all that time, he's never brought anyone to the house. Oh, we've met a couple of his dates, but he'd never bring them home. No one seems to last more than a week at the most."

"Well, maybe he's just not into commitment. You know, like a fuck 'em and leave 'em kind of guy. Not that there's anything wrong with that," Malakai hurried to add.

Flynn smiled to himself at how hard Malakai was trying to defend their mate, but Flynn was starting to understand what the alpha was telling them.

"Look, I honestly don't know if he's lying or not, but he let something slip once that makes me think that his sex life isn't all he's made it out to be." Xander ran a hand through his hair and groaned. "You really should be talking to Jackson. They're the closest in age, and Jackson just has a way of making a person open up and spill their guts."

"Unless you're Talon," Braxton mumbled under his breath. He flushed a brilliant shade of scarlet when the table erupted into laughter. "Stupid shifter super-hearing."

"Just tell us what ya have to say, Xander." Flynn was itching to end the conversation and go find his mate. He really wasn't getting anything out of the talk that would help him anyway.

"I don't think he meant to say it, but Keeton asked him why he was being such an asshole one night, and Boston shot back that at least we'd gotten laid in the last eight years."

Flynn almost fell off his chair at the announcement. "Eight years?"

Xander shrugged. "I don't know. That's just what he said." He stared down at his hands where they were linked together on the table for a long time before he spoke again. "He was seeing this one guy a few months ago. I thought things were going pretty well."

"Spit it out," Malakai demanded. Flynn had to bite the inside of his cheek to keep from laughing at the little vampire's vehemence. Oh, he'd mated a feisty one.

"I don't know all the details, but I guess the guy was into biting. Boston freaked, one thing led to another, and someone called the cops. Logan showed up on the scene because they had reports of an injury. When he got there, the cops were trying to restrain Boston. The handcuffs went on, and Boston completely lost it."

"Did he fight them then?"

Braxton looked Flynn right in the eyes and shook his head. "He broke down. Screaming, crying, you name it. He didn't remember anything about it afterward." His gaze shifted to Malakai. "So, be careful with those fangs of yours. It would kill him if he hurt you, even by accident."

Words were said after that, but Flynn didn't hear them. All he could hear were the soft moans and whimpers that filled that cold basement he'd called home for three years. Most often, guards would come and escort them to one of the vampires that required their services. Sometimes, however, the vampires came to them. That's when the screams would start.

The vampires weren't gentle with those razor sharp teeth of theirs, either. They'd done all they could to inject as much humility and pain into their feedings as possible. There was only one way out of that basement—death.

Flynn still remembered the night that the guards came to him, all too eager to tell him that they'd done away with his little "pet." Since the vampires drank from them so often and rarely fed them, he'd been too weak to attempt to shift, but that hadn't stopped him from fighting with everything he had. The grief and pain fueled his rage, until he was a mindless, snarling imitation of himself.

The next thing he remembered was waking up naked and staked to a side of a barn. He felt a tiny twinge of guilt that he'd smudged the facts a bit when he told Boston. His mate didn't need all the gory details, though. They hadn't drained Flynn, but rammed huge pieces of wood into his shoulders and left him there to bleed to death.

"Flynn?"

Coming out of his memories, Flynn's heart broke at the tears streaming down Malakai's face. Gently brushing away the salty drops with his fingertips, he kissed both of Malakai's eyes before moving on to his mate's lips. "What has you so upset then, little one?" He may have only just met the vampire, but already he wanted nothing more than to slay the man's demons and keep him safe.

In answer, Malakai reached up and brushed away tears from Flynn's cheeks that he didn't even realize he'd cried. "I could ask you the same thing, Flynn. What were you thinking?"

"Unpleasant thoughts, sweetheart. Ones we'll not be discussin' just yet." Flynn thanked Xander and Braxton then stood, pulling Malakai to his feet as well. "I'm thinkin' our mate might need some special lovin' just now."

Malakai's eyes softened, and he brushed his hand over Flynn's chest. "I think he might not be the only one."

Truer words, he'd never heard, but he'd work on healing Boston before he worried about himself. Judging from the dark circles under Malakai's eyes, and the paleness of his skin, his little mate was in need of some healing of his own. "Ya need to drink, little one."

"I'll be fine for now," Malakai whispered. "It's not so bad."

Flynn sighed in frustration. Why fate had seemed fit to bless him with two of the most stubborn men on the planet, he'd never know. Instead of arguing, he just took Malakai's hand and pulled him toward the house. He had no intentions of letting his man starve, but he didn't look in danger of keeling over just yet.

"We'll figure it out," Malakai whispered.

Flynn hoped he was right, but he couldn't help but have his doubts.

* * * *

Mumbling angrily under his breath as he paced his bedroom, Boston felt like the biggest sack of shit on the planet. Part of him wanted to rush back out that door, scoop Malakai into his arms, and lick every inch of his skin. Another part of him wanted to run out that same door, and just keep running—pretend like he'd never met the man.

He was pissed off at fate for giving him a vampire for a mate. He was pissed off at Malakai for being a vampire. But most of all, he was pissed off at himself for being a weak, sniveling idiot that couldn't get past the fact that his mate had fangs. Malakai and Flynn deserved so much better than him. They deserved a mate who was whole.

Learning the circumstances of Flynn's perceived betrayal didn't just wipe away all the feelings Boston had been harboring for the last eight years. He couldn't flip a switch and make it all disappear overnight no matter how badly he wished he could. Besides, there was also the little fact that Flynn hadn't bothered to try to find him in all those years.

He still had nightmares about the time spent in Montana. Though he'd grown up a lot since then, there was still a small part of him that felt like a scared little boy, constantly looking over his shoulder, and waiting to be dragged back to that horrible place.

Ever since they'd blown the lid wide open on Cyrus Redway's shady dealings, the nightmares had increased in frequency and intensity. Would the vampires who'd held him know that he'd survived? Would they come looking for him? He wasn't too proud to admit that the idea scared the shit out of him. To add to that, he now had two mates to protect. It didn't matter that Malakai was a vampire as well, he was still fair game for those sick and demented bastards.

Maybe he should leave. Watching Flynn and Malakai interact, Boston knew they were made for each other. They just fit the way mates should. Not like him. He didn't fit. Flynn would take care of

Malakai, and Malakai would never let Flynn want for anything. Hell, they probably wouldn't even miss Boston.

With that thought in mind, he hurried over to his closet and pulled out an old tattered backpack. He wouldn't need much. By the time he'd carried the bag back to his bed, he'd been busted, though.

"Goin' somewhere, are ya?" Flynn's smooth voice asked as he stepped into the room behind Malakai. "And where is it ya think ya be runnin' to, Boston Mackey?"

Boston didn't answer. No matter what he said, he'd still end up being the coward or the bad guy. Nope, it was better to just keep his mouth shut.

"Boston?" Malakai stepped a little farther into the room. It was obvious from his puffy, red-rimmed eyes that he'd been crying. The knowledge only served to make Boston feel like a bigger asshole.

He wanted to say something to comfort the vamp. He wanted to promise all sorts of things, but he'd already broken too many in just the last hour for that.

"Malakai needs to feed," Flynn said out of the blue. "Would ya like to stay?"

"Stay? Stay for what?" *To watch his mate feed off of someone else? No thank you.*

Flynn rolled his eyes as if he found Boston completely stupid. Then he shrugged his jacket off and began rolling up one sleeve on his pristine white shirt. Walking over to the bed, he settled on the end of the mattress and rested his bare forearm on his thigh. "I am sorry for this," he said, nodding with a quick glance at Boston. "I'm not thinkin' I'm ready for the neck."

Liar. Flynn didn't want to make Boston uncomfortable. It was written all over his handsome face.

Malakai, on the other hand, looked so scared, Boston thought the man was going to pass out. He looked between Flynn's wrist and Boston's face several times before he started shaking his head. "No. That's okay. I'm fine. I don't need it."

"Would ya take it from someone else? I'm not sure how the mates would be feelin' about that, but I could ask."

"No," Boston heard himself snarl. What kind of man was he if he couldn't even give his mate what he needed to survive? "I'll do it."

This only appeared to frighten Malakai further. "No, no. I'm fine. Really. You're not ready for that, Boston. Please."

Well, that did it. His pride piqued, Boston sat down beside Flynn and unbuttoned his collar, pulling it to the side and tilting his head. If he was going to do this, he might as well jump in headfirst.

A strong hand landed on his thigh, and Boston turned to find Flynn looking at him in concern. "No. I can feel ya shakin', Boston. Ya not need to do this to prove anything."

He was wrong, though. The minute Flynn had suggested that Malakai drink from someone else, Boston had wanted to rip his pack brothers apart. No one should ever feel Malakai's mouth on them besides Boston and Flynn. If he couldn't give Malakai up, then he needed to learn to accept the man for everything he was.

"He's right, Boston. I don't know everything about what happened to you, but I do know that you have no reason to feel ashamed. I understand why you don't want me to bite you. It doesn't hurt me. I just want you to feel safe and happy."

God, now the guy was comforting him. Malakai was practically vibrating where he stood, obviously needing the blood Boston could give him, and *he* was comforting *Boston*. If that wasn't enough to make a man feel like a failure, Boston didn't know what was.

"I can't let you go, Malakai." Boston didn't realize how true the words were until he said them out loud. "So, with that being the case, I'm going to have to get used to those fangs of yours sooner or later."

"I vote for later," Malakai said, and his voice cracked twice. "We're just getting to know each other. There is no reason you should trust me with something this important. I'll be fine for a few more days, and we can revisit this discussion then. Okay?"

"I'll just be gettin' your room set up," Flynn mumbled under his breath, and Boston was grateful that the man understood that he needed a moment alone with Malakai.

Stretching his neck, he placed a soft kiss on Flynn's rough cheek. "Thank you, sweetheart."

"Always for you," Flynn whispered back. He pecked Boston's lips and rose from the bed. Kissing Malakai on the way out, he disappeared through the door without another word.

"Come here, Malakai." Boston held his arms open and wiggled his fingers.

Malakai hesitated for a long time, but eventually, he shuffled across the carpet and stood between Boston's spread thighs. With a mischievous smile, Boston wound his arms around that tiny waist and pulled his mate into his lap. "There, that's better."

Malakai's giggle cut off, and his beautiful face flushed. "Oh, hell, I cannot believe I just did that."

Boston thought it was adorable. "Flynn is going to set up Jackson's old room for you with blackout curtains. The bed is too small for us to all fit in there, but we'd be happy to sleep on the floor if you don't want to be alone."

"No." Malakai shook his head quickly. "I'll be fine. I've slept by myself for a very long time. You and Flynn need some time alone anyway." He reached up carefully and cradled Boston's face in his palms. "Let him in, Boston. That man loves you so much that it's nauseating."

"I'm hurting him," Boston whispered. "I don't want to hurt him. I just don't know how to be any different." It was probably the hardest confession of his life.

"Let him show you."

His first time with his mates should include them both. Boston wasn't sure how he felt about letting Flynn love on him with Malakai in the other room. "Do you want to stay?"

Malakai smiled sweetly and pecked at his lips. "I'm not jealous, big guy. And as much as I would love to watch you two together, you need to make things right with Flynn on your own." He held his hand up when Boston started to speak. "I don't need to know all the details right now. You'll tell me when you feel more comfortable with me. Just know that I understand, and I want you to be happy."

"It feels wrong."

Malakai laughed. "Oh, Boston, there is nothing wrong with loving your mate. There is a lot of history between you and Flynn. You've only just met me. I don't expect you to have those same feelings for me."

"It still feels wrong," Boston pouted. Why couldn't he just get his shit together?

Brushing their lips together, Malakai chuckled. "Do you want me?"

"Definitely," Boston confessed, grinding his cotton-covered erection against Malakai's ass. "You are sexy as fuck. How could anyone not want you?"

"Then don't worry. I want to know that if things don't work out between us, that you'll have Flynn to take care of you. I promise that it doesn't hurt me or make me feel left out. I know you want me. We'll get there in our own good time."

"How can you be so understanding?" Boston felt like a heel, and Malakai trying to make it easier for him only drove the feeling home.

"I've waited a long time to find my mate. I'm willing to do whatever it takes to keep you and Flynn." He kissed Boston again before wiggling out of his lap. "Don't push him away, Boston. Not everyone gets a second chance."

Yet, Boston had been given two—one with Flynn, and one with Malakai. And he was still fucking it up.

Go me!

Chapter Eight

"Will I be sleepin' on the floor then?" Flynn shut the door quietly behind him as he entered Boston's room. He'd gotten Malakai settled and still felt a little shocked when the vampire confessed to him the conversation he'd had with Boston.

"No," Boston whispered. He hadn't moved from the end of the bed—right where he'd been sitting when Flynn left nearly twenty minutes earlier. "I'm sorry, Flynn."

"Ah, darlin', what do ya have to feel sorry about?" Flynn hurried over and knelt on the floor in front of his mate. "I won't be pressurin' ya for anything, but I would like to hold ya."

"It's not fair for me to hold something against you that you had no control over." Boston wouldn't look him in the eyes, and he spoke in a slow monotone that had Flynn worried. "I don't think I'm really angry at you, though. I think I'm pissed at myself because I couldn't stop it. I let them hurt you, and I have to live with that for the rest of my life. I already have so many things to be mad at myself about, and I guess you're just getting some of the overflow."

"Now ya listen to me," Flynn began.

Boston just kept talking, though. "When I saw you that night, I didn't understand how my heart could keep beating with so much pain. Even when you told me the truth of what happened, the pain didn't just magically disappear." He finally met Flynn's eyes, and the pain and fear there would have crumpled Flynn to the knees if he wasn't already there. "Why didn't you ever look for me? I know I sent you away, but why did you go so easily?"

"What would ya have me to do, Boston? I did search for ya. I'm an Enforcer, though, not a Tracker. I even petitioned The Council, but the old fools wouldn't tell me a bleedin' thing, now would they?"

"You looked for me?"

"Why do ya imagine I jump at the job when Blaise offered it to me? He wanted me to guard a pack of Moonlighters, he says. And I think maybe this be fate's way of givin' me another chance. I'm not knowin' what to expect when I get here, then ya come walkin' down the stairs, and I thought my heart would stop beatin', I did."

There were so many more things he wanted to say, but Boston chose that moment to launch himself off the bed and tackle Flynn to the floor. Their mouths crashed together as Boston squirmed on top of him, and all thoughts of conversation fled.

Flynn's cock went rock hard in seconds, swelling inside his boxers and testing the strength of his zipper. Fisting his hands in Boston's short, blond hair, he took over the kiss, rolling the man beneath him and pillaging the sweet depths of his mouth.

"Need you," Boston whimpered. "Tired of being numb. Make me feel something."

The words ripping at his heart, Flynn gentled his exploration of his lover's body. "Sex will not be makin' ya feel anything in here," He rested his palm over Boston's heart.

"It will if it's with you," Boston countered quietly. "I've loved you for almost eleven years. I've compared every man to you since then, and they all come up short. I don't want to be like this anymore. Please."

"Oh, *mo chroí*," Flynn breathed before pressing his lips back to Boston's. Sweet Jesus, he'd waited so many years to hear those words again. His feelings for the man beneath his hands hadn't faded over the years. It was all the proof he needed that though they'd been young, their love was real. No matter the distance and time that had separated them, Flynn had never found another to replace Boston in his heart.

After only a short time with Malakai, he had a feeling that his heart would be doing quite a bit of expanding, though. He couldn't replace Boston, but he could open up his heart and let Malakai in as well. He only hoped that in time, Boston could do the same.

Pushing away the doubts and uncertainty, he climbed to his feet and held a hand out to help Boston up. Without saying anything, he began undressing, never taking his eyes from his lover's dark blue gaze.

Boston, on the other hand, stripped out of his clothes, ripping them in some places in his haste, and dove onto the mattress. "Hurry," he growled.

Flynn laughed at the younger man's eagerness. "Patience, sweetheart. I promise to be takin' good care of ya."

"I know you will. I just want you to hurry up and do it."

Chuckling all the way to the nightstand, Flynn pulled the drawer open and rummaged around for something to ease the way. He wasn't a small man, and if what Xander said was true, it had been a while since anyone had taken Boston.

Finding a small, barelyused bottle of lube, Flynn wrapped his fingers around it and crawled onto the bed, covering his lover and pressing their chests together. The first feel of Boston's heated skin against his sent his dick throbbing and his head spinning.

"No talking," Boston panted, his hands roaming Flynn's body. "Just touch me. I've been dreaming about you touching me."

Never one to disappoint, Flynn took Boston's mouth in a possessive kiss as he stroked his lover's body, relearning every dip, valley, and curve. Larger, harder, Boston's body had filled out in all the right places since he was a scrawny teenager.

Flynn promised himself that he'd explore every one of the new muscles with his tongue another time. But just then, they were both too wound up with urgency for the slow and sensual exploration.

Panting and moaning, Boston rocked his hips, arching up into Flynn's body. Their hard cocks nestled together, sliding against each other like long lost lovers. Breaking away from Boston's mouth,

Flynn trailed his lips down his mate's throat, careful not to nip at the skin like he wanted to do. He wouldn't do anything to ruin this moment, not even unintentionally.

"Please, please, please," Boston chanted. Apparently, the rule of no talking only applied to Flynn. He could live with that.

Smiling against the damp skin covering Boston's collarbone, he popped the cap on the small bottle still clutched in his hand and poured a generous amount into his palm. Lifting up so that he could see into his lover's eyes, he coated both of their erections with the slippery liquid, loving the deep groan that rumbled in Boston's chest.

"More."

"So impatient."

"More," Boston growled.

Dipping his head to hide his smile, Flynn applied more lube to his fingertips and reached between their bodies to separate Boston's muscled globes. The first soft caress against his mate's hole almost made him purr. Boston's sweet pucker quivered under his touch, clenched and relaxed, practically begged him for more.

Boston whimpered quietly, spread his legs wider, and jerked Flynn down into another toe-curling kiss. Every brush of Boston's tongue set his blood on fire and made his cock pulse and jerk.

Letting the younger man control the kiss, Flynn gently inserted the tip of his finger into Boston's fluttering hole, groaning when the tight heat surrounded his digit. Boston snarled and threw himself into the mating of their lips and tongues with a wild abandon as his hips snapped upward.

Taking care with his love, Flynn wiggled his finger inside and stilled until the muscles began to relax and accept him. Then he pumped his finger gently, slowly, unwilling to hurt his mate for anything in the world.

Once he had the one finger gliding in and out of his lover with ease, he added a second, starting the process over and loosening Boston to accept him. By the time he slipped in a third finger, Boston was a writhing pile of mindless lust beneath him—just the way he wanted him.

Their slick cocks slid together, both leaking feely from the tips. Flynn's balls ached and his belly burned. Boston's scent filled his head, driving away every thought but the pleasure he was receiving just from loving on the man.

"Now," Boston pleaded. "Need you, Flynn."

Flynn couldn't agree more. Extracting his fingers, he lined up the head of his cock and pushed in so slowly that his body began to shake. When he was finally seated to the root, he thought he'd die from the overwhelming sensation of being inside his fated mate. God, it had been so long since he'd felt so complete, so at peace.

Unfortunately, he wasn't going to last long. Already he could feel the electricity zipping along his spine and the tightening of his sac. Thrusting his hips gently, he made love to the one man that had ever meant anything to him.

Boston's hands came up to cup his cheeks, and they stared into each other's eyes as they moved together. Flynn's eyes burned from the emotions that welled up inside him. His heart swelled until he thought it would explode, and everything faded away except the man beneath him.

The rhythm never increased, never picked up in tempo, but the intensity skyrocketed until Flynn thought his entire body would explode when he finally reached his climax. Then Boston released his face and turned his head to the side, baring his neck in the sweetest, most submissive gesture that Flynn had ever witnessed.

"Please, Flynn. Make me yours."

Knowing Boston's aversion to being bitten, the act was so full of trust and need that Flynn couldn't help the tears that brimmed over. Dipping his head, he licked at the salty skin between Boston's neck and shoulder, gasping when his canines elongated into sharp fangs.

Though he wasn't a carnivore, didn't have sharp teeth even when he shifted, his body seemed to know what was needed. Deciding not to question it, he scraped them over Boston's flesh, testing his mate's comfort zone.

When Boston only moaned and clutched at his shoulders, Flynn pushed his canines through the smooth skin as gently as possible. The first gush of his mate's blood over his tongue made him growl.

Continuing to thrust into his mate, Flynn pulled his canines free and licked over the small wound. Finally, Boston was his. Lost in the pleasure and the overwhelming scent of his mate—like thunderstorms and fresh peaches—he wasn't prepared when Boston gripped his hair and yanked his head to the side.

The small bite of pain he felt when Boston bit into his shoulder quickly subsided, leaving nothing but an intense pleasure that he could feel right down to his soul. The mating bond snapped into place like a rubber band, and Flynn roared as his cock exploded, filling Boston's dark depths with his seed.

Pulling his teeth from Flynn's shoulder, Boston threw his head back as his entire body tensed and his inner walls contracted around Flynn's still-spurting cock. "I love you!" he shouted, throwing his head back and gripping at Flynn's sides with a bruising hold.

Long, creamy ropes of semen erupted from Boston's slit, spraying the space between them with his essence. The look on his face was the most beautiful thing Flynn had ever seen, and he vowed to see that look again and again in the years to come.

"And I love you, *a ghrá*. I never stopped."

They lay there for a long time, just staring into each other's faces as they tried to slow their breathing and heart rates. "I didn't freak," Boston said, and he sounded proud of the fact, if a little shocked.

Flynn was definitely proud of his mate. "Do ya think ya can let Malakai in now, darlin'?"

Boston's face paled. "I wanted him with us, but he said no. Do you think he doesn't want me?"

"Aye, he be wantin' ya, Boston. Malakai is a good mate, and he just be givin' ya what ya needed. He's special."

The smile was slow, but it eventually stretched over Boston's face. "He is very special. I don't love him. I mean, how can I? I barely know him. But I can see myself falling so easily. He's perfect for us."

"Did ya doubt fate, my beauty?"

Boston snorted and pecked at Flynn's lips. "Not at all. I just needed to pull my head out of my ass. Should we go talk to him now?"

"I think he was wantin' to be alone for a bit. We can talk to him once he's rested."

Boston chewed his lip for a minute and nodded. "Okay. But I want to talk to him as soon as he wakes up. I've made a complete mess of things, and I need to apologize. He's so perfect, fangs and all. It kills me that I've fucked things up so much."

"Ya have a big heart, Boston Mackey." Flynn nuzzled his nose against his lover's throat as his softening cock slipped free of Boston's hole. "Just be you, and he'll love ya as much as I do."

Boston's arms wound around his back and held him tight. "I hope you're right."

"Aye, I'm always right."

"No, you're always an idiot." Boston chuckled and tightened his arms when Flynn tried to sit up. "But I love you anyway. I'm glad you're back. I missed you."

"Ya won't know what to be doin' with so much love. Me and the little vampire will be givin' ya all ya can handle and then some."

"Just don't give up on me."

"Never."

Chapter Nine

For the next three days, Malakai did everything in his power to avoid being alone with his mates. He pretended to sleep well past the time the sun had set. He went to bed early. He always made sure they were surrounded by pack members. It was fucking exhausting.

"Malakai?"

Shit! Malakai flew off his bed and jumped from foot to foot. Maybe if he didn't say anything, Boston would go away. Yes, that was a good plan. It always worked before.

"Malakai, I can hear you," Boston called through the door. He sounded totally exasperated. "Just open the damn door and talk to me."

Resigned to the inevitable, Malakai crossed the room and unlocked the door before opening for his mate. "You wanted to talk?" Good grief, was that his voice? It sounded like he'd been gargling nails. Well, he supposed that was appropriate considering his throat felt like that's exactly what he'd been doing. And why the hell couldn't Boston just stay in focus like a good mate?

"Fuck," Boston gasped, pushing his way into the room and jerking Malakai up into his arms. "This stops now."

"You're being a complete Neanderthal." Malakai wanted to sound haughty and indignant, but his words came out kind of slurred. "And would you please stop moving around so much? You're making my stomach hurt."

"Baby, we're sitting on the bed. I'm not moving at all."

"Oh, well, then I apologize."

Sighing heavily, Boston pulled Malakai to him and hugged him to his chest. His big hand slid down Malakai's back gently. Malakai whimpered at the contact—partly from pleasure, and partly because every part of his body hurt like the ten shades of hell.

"I can feel your goddamn bones, Malakai. What the hell is going on? Why are you hiding from me when you obviously need me and Flynn?"

"I'm fine."

"Stop lying to me, damn it!"

Malakai started trembling at the anger in the man's voice. "I'm sorry."

Boston sighed again and rubbed his cheek over the top of Malakai's head. "You need to feed."

Malakai just whimpered. This close, he was having a hard time not sinking his fangs into Boston's neck. Sweet baby Jesus, the man smelled like heaven. He was so thirsty. He whimpered again.

"Shh, baby. Just take what you need." Boston palmed the back of his head and urged him toward his neck. His muscles were tense, though, and Malakai could practically feel the anxiety rolling off him.

"No." He shook his head quickly, groaning when it exploded with pain and spots danced in his vision. "Flynn," he croaked.

"Flynn had to leave this morning. He won't be back until tomorrow. We wanted to tell you, but you're always hiding from us."

"I can wait." Even as he said the words, he found himself licking along the smooth column of Boston's throat. Snapping himself out of it, he jerked away so violently that he almost ended up on the floor. Luckily, his mate caught him, holding him firmly in his lap.

"Do you really hate me that much?"

Had anyone ever sounded more heartbroken? Malakai seriously doubted it. "No, I don't hate you. I can tell how uncomfortable you are. You don't want to do this, and I'm not going to force you." He dropped his chin to his chest before whispering, "I don't want *you* to hate *me*."

"Not going to happen," Boston said firmly. "Does it scare me a little? Absolutely. Is that going to stop me from doing the right thing? You bet your sweet ass it's not."

"Boston, please don't make me do this."

"Malakai. Shut the fuck up. You need to feed. If Stavion could see you now, he'd beat my ass, take you away, and I'd never see you again. And you know what?" His long fingers slid under Malakai's chin and tilted his head up. "I wouldn't blame him. In fact, I'd probably thank him. I have been one seriously shitty mate to you, but that stops now."

Well, what the hell did he say to that? Every part of him screamed that this would end badly, but he was so damn thirsty, and he just wanted the pain to stop. Deciding to take what was willingly offered and deal with the fallout later, he licked along Boston's neck again, groaning at the salty flavor of his mate. Then he stopped and pulled back to look into the man's face. "Would you prefer the wrist?"

Boston rolled his eyes and tilted his head to the side, stretching his neck to give Malakai better access. "Just do it."

Being as gentle as he possibly could, Malakai bent forward and let his fangs slide through Boston's flesh like a hot knife through butter. When Boston's blood filled his mouth, he instantly knew that he'd be addicted for life. Sucking greedily at the shifter's neck, he still remembered to keep things calm and gentle for his frightened mate.

Except, Boston didn't feel frightened. His muscles were still tense, but every draw on his neck had his hips thrusting up to rub the hard mound in his jeans against Malakai's naked ass. *Oops.* He'd completely forgotten he was nude.

He drank until the throbbing in his temples stopped, then relinquished his hold on Boston's neck and licked at the twin puncture wounds lazily. That's when his eyes focused on the bite mark right next to his. Instead of being jealous or hurt, the sight filled him with so much joy that tears sprang to his eyes.

Flinging his arms around Boston's neck, he squeezed his mate with all the strength he had. "I'm so happy for you! Flynn is a good mate."

"So are you, baby," Boston groaned raggedly.

It was only then that Malakai felt the damp denim grinding against his ass. "Did you come just from me biting you?"

"Yes." Boston flashed him a smile, proud and cocky. "Well, that and having this sexy little body rubbing against me." Then the smile faded away, and he became serious. "It was amazing. Thank you, Malakai."

"You know I didn't bond us, right?" Malakai blurted. "I mean, I'm not opposed to being your mate or bonding with you, but I didn't trick you or anything like that. I just wanted you to know that I would never do anything—"

Boston chuckled as his hand came up to cover Malakai's mouth. "Breathe, baby. It's okay. I know you didn't claim me. I'm not opposed to it either, but I think we should probably get to know each other a little better first."

Malakai nodded his head in agreement. The last thing he wanted was for them to bond, and then Boston and Flynn decide that they didn't want him. Boston's warm hands began roaming his nude body, and Malakai almost jumped out of his skin. He couldn't stop the moan that bubbled up in his chest if he'd wanted to, but this was such a bad idea.

Jumping up from Boston's lap like he'd been electrocuted, he backed away slowly and smiled. "You are gorgeous, and I can't even describe how much I want you. I can't think when you touch me, though."

"Mmm," Boston purred. "I don't want you to think."

"That's just it." Malakai squealed and jumped out of the way when Boston lunged for him. "It's instinctual to want to claim your mate, and it only gets worse when we're intimate. I think we should hold off on that." He tried to speak with conviction, but it was damn hard when he was running around the room, trying to dodge his mate's advances.

Boston stopped, fisted his hands on his hips, and cocked his head to the side. "Is that why you've been avoiding us?"

"Do you have any idea how hard it is to be in the same room with you two and not want to jump you? Add to the fact that I was so damn thirsty, and all I could think about was groping and biting every inch of you I could reach."

"No more," Boston growled, and Malakai was afraid he'd said something to piss off his big shifter. "You will not hurt yourself again just to please my neurotic ass. I think I just proved that I accept you for everything that you are. And even enjoyed it," he added with a glance down at the wet stain on the front of his jeans.

"I won't, I promise." Malakai swelled with happiness until he thought it would leak out of his ears. "I still want to hold off on the intimacy, though. Just for a little while, okay?"

Boston sighed, but dipped his head. "Okay. After all I've asked from you, I guess I have no right to complain. I guess I'll just go jump in the shower and fantasize about burying my cock in your tight little ass."

Though it was obvious Boston was trying to tempt him, the little pout on his lips just made Malakai want to giggle. "I'm sure you'll survive. You can always take your sexual frustrations out on Flynn."

"Oh, no." Boston shook his head adamantly. "If I can't have you, then he can't have me."

Malakai didn't understand that logic at all, so he just grinned stupidly. "If that's what you want."

"Of course that's not what I want, but for some reason, fate decided that I need two mates. And call me greedy, but I don't want just one. I'm willing to wait as long as you want, baby, but I won't feel right about fucking Flynn with you alone in the other room."

"I think that's beautiful," Malakai whispered. He cleared his throat and smiled again. "I have a feeling that our big, alpha mate isn't going to feel quite the same about it, though."

Boston winked over his shoulder before walking out the door.

"You just let me deal with Flynn Murphy."

* * * *

Four days later, Boston finally had a night off and planned to take full advantage of it. He didn't have a clue what he was doing, but he hoped his plan didn't backfire in his face.

They needed some time alone, and that's exactly what Boston planned to give his mates. There were too many distractions, too many interruptions in the house. He wanted a chance to get to know Malakai and relearn about Flynn without prying eyes and ears.

"Just a little farther," he called over his shoulder as they tramped through the trees. The place he was taking them still held bad memories, but he was hoping to change that. With any luck, they could make new memories and turn it into a special place for just them.

"Boston, where are we going?" Malakai squeaked as he tripped over a fallen log and fell headlong into Boston's back. "Oomph."

Spinning around and catching his mate before he could fall, Boston chuckled and set Malakai up straight. "Don't you have boots or something?" His eyes traveled over Malakai's thin sweater, down his dark slacks, and over the brown loafers. "This probably isn't the most practical thing to wear in the woods, baby."

Malakai flushed and looked down at the ground. "I don't have anything else. I don't spend a lot of time outside. Nature and I don't really get along."

"I like it," Flynn said casually as he took Malakai's hand and pulled him along. "Ya look sexy, and it be fittin' for ya."

Malakai smiled adoringly up at Flynn, and Boston melted into a puddle of sappy goo. "He's right. I wasn't making fun of you, Malakai. I love the way you look."

Shaking his head, Malakai took Boston's hand and brought it to his lips, melting Boston further. "You're right. If I'm going to be mated to two shifters, I should have more appropriate clothing for hiking and such. Maybe you could help me find something on your next night off."

"Absolutely."Boston was quickly beginning to realize that he'd give his mates anything they wanted.

Stepping into the clearing, he released Malakai's hand and took the blanket from Flynn to spread over the ground. "Okay, clothes off."

Malakai's eyes rounded, and he started shaking his head as he took a couple of slow steps backward. "Boston, I don't think that's a good idea."

"Malakai, relax. We're just going to play. No sex, nothing to make you uncomfortable—it's just fun."

He still looked hesitant, but Malakai slowly pulled his thin, beige sweater over his head. Boston tried not to groan, determined to keep his promise, but damn, the man was gorgeous.

His pale skin almost glowed in the moonlight as it stretched tight across his lean muscles. His ebony hair stood out in stark contrast, falling elegantly over one eye, and seriously testing Boston's self-control.

Wrenching his gaze away when Malakai reached for the fastener on his slacks, Boston's eyes settled on Flynn. He almost choked before he burst into laughter. Flynn was completely naked, flexing his muscles and making the most ridiculous faces. Then he lifted his arms and curled his hands inward in a classic muscleman pose before kissing each of his bulging biceps.

The cutest giggle he'd ever heard had him whipping back to Malakai. The man had a hand over his mouth, his eyes dancing with mirth as he watched Flynn act a fool. Then the giggles flowed into a chuckle and soon Malakai was clutching his ribs as he howled in laughter.

"Yes, very intimidating," Boston said around his snort. He couldn't pull his eyes away from Malakai, though. He was completely breathtaking when he smiled, and his laughter was the sweetest song Boston had ever heard. He wanted to hear it again. Jerking a thumb at Flynn, he rolled his eyes. "He's a big marshmallow."

Malakai fell into another fit of laughter, and it was so infectious that Boston couldn't help but join in.

"I was thinking more like a Twinkie," Malakai said when he'd regained some of his composure.

Boston tilted his head to the side and considered the big shifter. "Is that because he's all squishy on the inside?"

Malakai shrugged, but the corners of his lips twitched. "Not really. I just like Twinkies."

* * * *

Flynn crossed his arms over his chest and glared playfully at his mates. They were ganging up on him. Malakai had a quirky sense of humor, and the sounds of his mates' laughter made Flynn's heart swell with happiness.

It also made him shrivel with guilt. He knew he needed to tell them about the meeting he'd had with The Council. Things were going so well, though, and he didn't want to rock the boat when they were just getting to know each other.

He already knew what Boston's reaction would be, and the longer he put it off, the worse it would be. From what he'd learned about Malakai, he had a feeling that his little mate wouldn't react to the news any better than Boston. He'd have to tell them soon.

Boston had planned the night especially for them, though. Flynn wouldn't do anything to ruin it. Besides, maybe if they had a little fun, his mates would be in better moods when he told them.

"Okay, so what's the plan?" Malakai asked, his hands fisting on his hips as he rocked from side to side. The motion caused his half-hard cock to sway between his legs, and Flynn bit the inside of his cheek to keep from growling in desire. Sweet heavens, the little man looked good enough to eat. The two most gorgeous men on the planet, and they belonged to him. Flynn was one lucky son of a bitch.

"Well, I thought we could play hide and seek."

Flynn's eyebrows drew together, and he looked down at his own naked cock. "And would ya be tellin' me why we're needin' to be naked for it?"

Boston grinned widely and shrugged. "Everything is more fun naked."

"Here, here!" Malakai shouted and pumped his fist into the air. "I want to go first."

"Hidin' or seekin'?"

Malakai looked at Flynn and wiggled his eyebrows. "You hide. I'll bet you a blow job that I can find you in less than sixty seconds."

"Hey!" Boston crossed his arms over his chest and tried to look intimidating. The affect was lost a little by the twinkling in his eyes and swelling cock between his thighs. "What about me?"

Malakai reached up and patted the man on the shoulder. "Oh, don't worry, honey. I plan to find you, too." He looked over his shoulder and winked at Flynn. "That is unless you're afraid you'll lose."

"I'm not afraid of anything."

"Are you sure about that?" Malakai walked around Boston slowly. "Maybe you're...yella. Maybe you're a...chicken." Then he clucked and bobbed his head like a chicken.

Boston's eyes went wide, shock written all over his face. Flynn understood the feeling. They'd yet to see this side of their mate. Between Malakai strutting around and squawking like an infernal rooster, and the look of disbelief on Boston's face, it was too much for Flynn.

He started laughing and couldn't stop. He laughed so hard, his legs gave out, and he fell to the ground with his arms wrapped around his midsection.

"Oh, forget this," Boston finally said. He reached down and

cupped his cock and balls. "I'm taking my ball and going home. I don't want to play with you two anymore."

Flynn laughed harder at Boston's antics, then thought he'd pee himself when Malakai stuck his hips out and shook them back and forth, causing his dick to slap against his thighs. "Okay, but I still have the bat."

Then they were all on the ground, rolling around and clinging to each other like a bunch of idiots. It was the most fun Flynn had had in ages. He'd be thankful every day for the second chance he'd been given at happiness.

"Okay," Malakai panted a long time later. "Are you going to hide or not?"

"A blow job is the wager, right?"

Malakai nodded at Boston. "If I find you in under a minute, I get a blow job."

"And if we're winnin', we'll be getting' those blow jobs." Flynn wanted to be certain on this fact and work out any loopholes, because he definitely planned to win.

Malakai grinned mischievously. "But not until the end of the week. That's my rule." He suddenly became very serious. "I don't want to screw this up. I just want a few more days without sex getting in the way."

Flynn and Boston exchanged glances and nodded their agreement. "Whatever ya need," Flynn answered solemnly. As much as he ached to bury himself inside his mates, he would go as slow as Malakai needed.

"Okay, then." Malakai looked down at his watch, the only thing he was still wearing. "Sixty seconds to hide, then sixty to find you. Go!"

Flynn and Boston darted into the trees, separating and looking for a place to hide. Flynn ended up behind a mid-sized boulder, crouching low and peeking around it to watch for his mate.

His eyebrows drew together, and he frowned when he saw Boston standing right out in the open. What on earth was the man doing?

Malakai came darting through the trees and barreled right into Boston's chest. Boston caught the man and swung him up in his arms to plant a searing kiss on his mouth. "You found me."

Flynn chuckled under his breath and rose from his hiding place. He adored these men. His eyes drifted to Malakai's rock-hard cock, and his chuckle turned into a tortured groan.

Maybe winning wasn't so important. He'd give anything to have his lips wrapped around the impressive length just then. Sprinting up to his men, he grabbed Malakai up and kissed him just as passionately as Boston had.

"Aye, and ya be findin' me as well."

* * * *

Boston didn't know how much more he could take. His damn dick felt like it was going to fall off. For an entire week, he'd done exactly as Malakai had asked. It didn't matter that every fiber of his being was calling out for his mates. He held himself in check, and tried his damndest to be what Malakai needed. After their night spent playing in the woods, it was even harder, but he'd made a promise.

They'd talked and talked until his throat felt raw. Every new thing he learned about Malakai had him falling just a little more for the man. There was just something so giving about the vampire. Boston dared anyone who'd met him not to adore him.

Malakai had taken blood from both him and Flynn twice during the week. Boston hadn't been able to contain his mirth when Flynn had the exact same reaction as he had the first time. The man went off like a bottle rocket the instant Malakai had bitten into his neck. While it was sexy as fuck, the dazed look on Flynn's face had been hilarious.

Their little mate was sweet and affectionate, very giving with cuddles and kisses. He still refused to sleep in their room, though, and he hadn't budged on his position of no sex. While Boston understood

Malakai's reasoning behind holding off on the claiming, his body still desired his mate with an intensity close to pain. Something had to give and damn soon.

"My dick's going to fall off," Flynn whimpered as he stepped into the bedroom.

Boston chuckled, but there wasn't much humor in it. "I know the feeling." Oh, it would be so easy to fall into bed with Flynn and take the edge off, but he'd meant what he'd told Malakai. He didn't feel right about heating up the sheets with Flynn while Malakai was feeling the same clawing need as they were.

He'd explained it all to Flynn when the man had returned from his trip to The Council. Thankfully, Flynn had agreed. It wasn't that they could never have sex unless all three of them were together. Until Malakai felt comfortable with them enough to share his body, however, it just felt wrong.

"Aye, but ya haven't seen him in the shower all slippery and wet, now have ya?" Flynn flopped back on the bed and groaned. "Was a sight to behold."

"What!" Boston rolled over until he hovered above Flynn. "Why were you in the shower with him?"

"Ah, is someone jealous, my darlin'?"

"You bet your sexy ass I'm jealous. I want to be in the shower with him."

Flynn threw his head back and laughed. "I've not been in the shower with the little vamp, Boston. Just had my head up my arse and walked in on him."

"I can think of something else to put up your arse," Boston teased as he ground his groin against Flynn's. "Maybe we can seduce him? Or, hell, I just want to suck his cock. If we make it all about him, maybe he won't worry about us accidently claiming him. Besides, we both owe him. He did find us in under a minute after all." Boston wiggled his eyebrows suggestively.

"Now, that's a fine idea. Let's have us a kiss and go find our mate."

Rolling his eyes, Boston bent forward and kissed his mate with all the pent-up desire he'd been holding back for days. "Now can we go seduce Malakai?"

"As you wish." Flynn winked and patted Boston's hip. "I have a plan, if ya be wantin' to hear it."

Judging from the wicked gleam in Flynn's eyes, Boston definitely wanted to hear it. Once Flynn spelled it out for him, Boston couldn't wait to put it into action.

Chapter Ten

Still working to tame his body's reaction to Flynn seeing him naked in the shower, Malakai rushed down the hall with only a towel slung low on his hips. Hurrying into his room, he closed the door behind him and turned around, only to squeak when he found Flynn sitting on his bed.

"W–What are you doing h–here?" he stuttered.

Without saying anything, Flynn rose from the bed and began walking a slow circle around him. "Ya want him."

Huh? "Huh?"

"Boston. Ya want him."

Flynn's voice was quiet but hard. Had Malakai missed something? Was the shifter jealous? Had he and Boston talked and decided that they were better off without him? It wouldn't be the first time Malakai had been shunted to the side. "I…uh." It wasn't intelligent. Hell, it was barely coherent, but Malakai just didn't know what to say.

"I've seen that way ya look at him." Flynn's voice washed over him, making him shiver. God, he wished he had something more covering him than a towel. "Aye, I've seen the fire in those eyes of yours."

"I…don't." Malakai closed his eyes and swallowed hard. He wasn't denying that he was fiercely attracted to Boston. He had two of the most gorgeous mates on the planet. No, his statement had been a plea. *Please don't send me away.*

Flynn stopped behind him and moved closer, molding himself to Malakai's back. His fingers skimmed down Malakai's chest and right over the towel. He parted the fabric slowly, revealing the throbbing erection hiding there. Then those warm fingers wrapped around his length and squeezed him gently. "This says ya do."

Of course Flynn would have misunderstood his words. Malakai didn't know why, but in that moment, he got pissed. "Yes, I want him!" he snarled. "I want you both so much it hurts. Is that what you wanted to hear?"

Flynn chuckled, his warm breath fanning over the side of Malakai's neck. "Aye, my darlin'. That's what I've been needin' to hear." He gave the towel a little tug until it fell from Malakai's waist to pool on the floor around his feet. "If I promise not to claim ya, will ya give me what I need?"

"I'll give you anything," Malakai replied honestly.

"Thank fuck," came a breathy reply.

Malakai jumped a little when he opened his eyes to find Boston standing in front of him, gloriously naked and cock in hand. Licking his lips, he whimpered just a little at all the smooth, tanned skin on display. "Please," he begged. While he may not be ready to take that final plunge and bind them together eternally, he desperately needed to feel his mates.

His eyebrows drew together in confusion when he reached for Boston, only to have the man grab his wrists to prevent him. "This is all for you, baby. Whatever you want with no pressure. Just let us take care of you." He gave Malakai a little smirk. "We owe you, remember?"

Yes, oh, yes, Malakai remembered, and he fully intended to collect.

Boston leaned down to nip at his lips then flicked his tongue out to sooth the slight sting. His hands and mouth left a trail of liquid heat down Malakai's chest and abs as he slowly lowered to his knees.

Flynn's hands replaced Boston's mouth, roaming his chest and stopping only occasionally to tug at his nipples while he continued to lick and suck at Malakai's neck and shoulders. Closing his eyes and dropping his head back to Flynn's shoulder, Malakai moaned loudly when wet heat engulfed the head of his cock, and a slippery tongue began probing at his slit.

"So good," he panted, thrusting his hips to push his aching dick farther into his lover's mouth. Another strangled groan fell from his lips when Boston swallowed him to the root, massaging the crown of his cock with his throat muscles.

Okay, he could definitely learn to live with having two big, sexy shifters loving on him. He imagined he might even crave it after this. How long could he continue to fight against them when they made him feel so good? While the things they were doing to his body were beyond amazing, it was the warmth in his heart that would prove to be his downfall if his men ever decided to leave him. It wouldn't be long before they tore down every wall, wormed their way inside, and took up residence.

A slick finger pushed through his ass cheeks and zeroed in on his clenching hole, driving all negative thoughts from his mind. Deciding to focus on the pleasure and worry about the bad stuff later, he rocked back against the digit until it pushed inside his greedy ass.

"Yesss," he hissed. "More. Please, I need more."

"Will ya come for me then, Malakai? Will ya scream for me?"

"Yes. Anything! Please!" He snapped his hips faster, fucking Boston's mouth while Flynn's finger sawed in and out of his tunnel.

"Then come for me," Flynn growled, curling his finger and pegging Malakai's prostate.

Like a trained puppy, Malakai squeezed his eyes closed and screamed loud enough to shake the walls as his cock discharged in Boston's mouth, pouring his seed down his mate's throat.

Boston moaned his approval, sucking him harder until he'd gained every drop that Malakai had to give. Flynn eased his finger from Malakai's fluttering asshole, and Boston bathed his flagging cock, licking him clean. Malakai had never felt more sated or cared for. "Thank you," he whispered.

"I don't want to sleep without you anymore," Boston murmured, nuzzling his cheek against the inside of Malakai's thigh. "Please, baby. Let us stay."

Flynn hummed his agreement, peppering little kisses down the side of Malakai's throat. "Please," he whispered.

"Not fair," Malakai whined. "You know I can't possibly say no when you beg like that."

Boston looked up at him and smirked. "I know." Rising up on his knees, he pressed kisses over Malakai's belly. "I need to hold you, though. Thank you, baby."

"Aye, thank you," Flynn mumbled reverently.

Why the men were thanking him, Malakai couldn't comprehend. They had practically giftwrapped happiness and presented it to him with a pretty bow. "Let me take care of you," he said, motioning toward Boston's pulsing erection.

His lover smiled and shook his head. "I'm better than fine. I meant it when I said this was all about you."

With a contended sigh, he bent from the waist, smirking as his ass pressed into Flynn's groin and the big shifter groaned. Then he pressed his lips to Boston's and delved his tongue inside for a taste of his man. "Okay, you can stay."

Turning quickly when he felt Flynn's hands groping at his ass, Malakai threw his arms around the man's neck and kissed him silly. He started to tell Flynn that he could stay as well, but yelped instead when Boston nipped at his ass. "Hey!"

"Sorry," Boston said, not sounding sorry in the least. "It was right there. I couldn't resist."

Rolling his eyes at his mate's antics, he turned back to Flynn and sighed. "Are you ever going to tell me why you were called to The Council?"

That seemed to get Boston's attention, because he shot to his feet and crossed his arms over his chest. "Yeah, I would like to know as well."

"I'll be goin' away for a few days."

"Where?" Malakai asked curiously.

Boston, on the other hand, growled. "You promised you wouldn't take any more assignments!"

Releasing Flynn, Malakai backed away until he felt Boston press up behind him. His mate's long arms slithered around him, holding him tightly. "Why, Flynn? Why are you taking this assignment?"

"I need to do this." Flynn didn't look angry, but he didn't look like he was going to budge either.

"When do you leave?" Boston still sounded pissed.

"Tomorrow."

Malakai's hand flew to his mouth, and he gasped. Boston snarled. "You weren't even going to tell us, were you?"

"I would have before morning."

"You've known for a week," Malakai said, trying to understand Flynn's perspective. He wasn't doing a good job of it, though. He agreed with Boston. Flynn shouldn't have kept something like that from them. "Why didn't you tell us sooner?"

Flynn looked into Boston's eyes as he spoke. "The Council is offerin' the job to me first. I need ya to understand, Boston."

"No!" Boston shouted loud enough to hurt Malakai's ears. His arms tightened like steel bands around Malakai's chest until he started having trouble breathing.

"Boston, calm down." The arms around him loosened, but Boston still kept a firm hold on him as though he was afraid Malakai would disappear if he didn't.

"You can't go. Tell them no."

"Ya know I'm needin' to do this."

"What the hell is going on?" Malakai demanded.

"The Council is bringing charges against the vampire coven that held us in Montana," Boston said dejectedly. "Flynn is going to bring them into custody."

Malakai's first instinct was to drop to his knees and beg Flynn not to go. Looking into Flynn's face and seeing the stubborn set of his jaw, he knew it wouldn't do any good. Flynn needed to do this—not only for himself, but for Boston as well. Malakai might not know the entire story, but he could understand that much.

Besides, the man was an Irish Thoroughbred shifter. He might not have teeth and claws, but he was massive when he shifted. Hell, at six-foot-four, the man was massive in his human form. Flynn was also well trained as an Enforcer, and Malakai doubted The Council would be stupid enough to send the man on the mission alone. "Who's going with you?"

"Raven, Varik, and a few others I'm not knowin'."

Raven would watch Flynn's back and make sure he made it home safely. "Be careful," Malakai finally whispered. Easing out of Boston's arms, he crossed the small space to Flynn and curled into the man's chest. "Please, be careful."

"I hate this." Boston pushed a hand through his hair and sighed before crossing over to press against Malakai's back again. His arms went around them, and Malakai glanced up to see his mates share a tender kiss. "If you get yourself killed, I'm going to kick your ass."

Burying his face into Flynn's chest, Malakai squeezed him tightly. "That goes double for me." Another thought struck him, and he jerked away so fast that the back of his head bounced off of Boston's chest. "You claimed Boston!" If Flynn died, Boston would as well, and Malakai would be left all alone to grieve the loss of both his mates. "Claim me."

"No," Boston said firmly.

Malakai spun around to look up at his mate. "You don't want me?"

Boston rolled his eyes and sighed. "Don't be stupid. Of course I want you. I know why you're doing this, though. Nothing is going to happen to me and Flynn." He cupped Malakai's cheek and kissed his forehead. "You're not ready, yet."

"He's right," Flynn agreed, kissing the top of Malakai's head. "Try not to worry for me. I'll be home before ya can miss me."

Famous last words. They'd yet to have anything work out the way they'd planned it.

Chapter Eleven

"It's been four days. Are you worried? I'm not really worried, but I'm kind of worried. Maybe we should call him. Have you tried to call him? Has he called you?"

Boston cut Malakai's rambling off with a kiss. "Calm down, baby. If something was wrong, Stavion would call us. No, Flynn hasn't called, but I'm not worried."

Malakai's lower lip poked out adorably. "Okay, if you say so."

"Come here." Boston settled back into the cushions on the sofa and held his arms open.

Malakai tilted his head to the side and cocked an eyebrow. "You do realize that I am a grown man, right? I'm even older than you."

"Fine. Then I'll sit in your lap." He started to sit up, but Malakai rolled his eyes and maneuvered over so that he perched on Boston's thighs. "See, now isn't it easier to just give me what I want?" he asked, winding his arms around Malakai's chest and holding him tightly.

Malakai snuggled into his arms, skimming his nose over the sensitive skin on Boston's throat. "Is it wrong that I like this?"

"Not at all. I like it, too." Sighing happily, Boston realized just how much he liked holding Malakai in his arms. Their mating had gotten off to a rocky start, but he couldn't even express how grateful he was that Malakai had been willing to give him a second chance.

All of his fears and doubts hadn't disappeared overnight, but he was trying. With Flynn off to save the world, Boston had been spending every free moment he had with his little vampire mate. Malakai was funny, sweet, and so damn smart. Boston could listen to him talk forever.

While every part of him yearned to claim Malakai and bond them together, he didn't think either of them were ready for that kind of commitment. He adored everything he'd learned about Malakai, but he still didn't know the man that well. A nasty little voice in the back of his head argued that he still held Malakai's vampiric nature against him. As much as he wanted to deny it, he knew it was true.

He hated himself for the way he felt. Malakai didn't deserve that kind of prejudice. He was nothing like the sadistic assholes who'd tortured Boston for years. Still, old habits die hard, and he'd spent most of his adult life loathing vampires. Just because his mate happened to be one didn't mean he could shut those feelings off and reprogram after only a couple of weeks.

He didn't hold anything against Malakai personally, but until he could get over his dislike of the race as a whole, he couldn't claim the man. It wouldn't be fair to either of them.

"You ready, kid?"

Glancing up at Talon, Boston nodded once. He hated going to work and leaving Malakai alone. "Give me a minute."

"Make it quick, or we're going to be late."

"Talon, quit being a douche and get your ass in here," Jackson called from the kitchen.

Boston couldn't stop his smile as Talon grunted and hurried out of the room. Did Flynn and Malakai have that kind of power over him? Would he do whatever they asked to make them happy? Staring down at the gorgeous man in his arms, he thought they just might. "I don't want to leave you," he confessed, rubbing his cheek over the top of Malakai's head.

"You have to work, Boston. I'll be just fine here on my own." Malakai tilted his head up to kiss the underside of Boston's jaw. "I'll miss you while you're gone."

Boston melted, his insides filling with warmth and sunshine. "You are so special," he whispered. It was the closest he could get to voicing his feelings. He was still so damn confused when it came to Malakai. All he really knew was that he didn't want to lose the man. "Xander and Logan are working tonight as well, but Jackson will be here. Braxton and Keeton, too, though I don't think they'd be much help in keeping you safe."

Malakai snorted. "Boston, I am perfectly capable of taking care of myself. Now, please, don't worry."

Skimming his hands down Malakai's ribs, Boston inhaled the sweet fragrance of his mate. His cock twitched with interest, taking notice of the firm ass nestled against his groin. "Maybe I could call in sick," he whispered huskily. Other than the one time he and Flynn had ambushed Malakai in his room, he'd yet to be intimate with the man. "I want you."

No matter that his emotions were a tangled mess, he couldn't help how his body responded to Malakai's nearness. He missed Flynn with something akin to pain. He knew Malakai felt the same. They should be comforting one another in their mate's absence, not tap-dancing around each other. Boston was so afraid he'd screw everything up, and Malakai was terrified of doing anything to make Boston uncomfortable.

"I need you," Boston clarified. It went well beyond want. He needed the peace and contentment that only his mate could give him. Ghosting his lips up the side of Malakai's neck, he imagined sinking his canines into the supple flesh and letting Malakai's rich blood bathe his tongue.

To his surprise, instead of fear, the images made him moan and his cock swell inside his tight jeans. This was *right*. He was an idiot for trying to fight it. "Please, baby."

Disappointment settled over him when Malakai flew out of his lap and shook his head. Dropping his head like a whipped dog, Boston sighed. He couldn't push Malakai. He couldn't force the man to want him. "I'm sorry."

"Stop," Malakai panted, causing Boston to snap his head up and peer intently at the vampire. "Don't be sorry. I want you." Malakai rubbed his palm over the impressive bulge behind his zipper and groaned. "Sweet mercy, I want to lick every inch of you. You have to work, though. There will be time to play when you get home."

Boston shot up from the couch, wrapped his mate up in his arms and spun him around. "You mean it?"

"Yes, I mean it. I'm tired of fighting you." Malakai's arms and legs snaked around him, and he bent closer until their lips rubbed against each other. "I'll be waiting for you."

With a pathetic whimper, Boston fisted his hand in Malakai's hair, jerking the man to him and mashing their lips together in a possessive kiss. "How the hell am I supposed to work with a hard-on?" he pouted.

Malakai winked and pecked at his lips again. "Very carefully."

"Stop sucking his face, and let's go," Talon grumbled as he walked into the room.

With a roll of his eyes, Boston kissed his mate one last time and put Malakai on his feet. "I'll be home as soon as I can."

Malakai smiled beautifully. "I look forward to it."

* * * *

After arguing with himself for a good hour, Malakai finally sucked up his courage and dialed Raven's cell phone number. Intense relief flooded through him when the Enforcer's deep voice answered on the third ring.

"Hey, man, and what do I owe the pleasure?"

"Raven, are you okay? Is Flynn with you? Please tell me what's going on."

"Everyone is safe. There have been some...complications. We've had to fall back and regroup. We think we have a strategy now, though, and we're going back in tomorrow night."

Malakai's blood ran cold. He didn't like the sound of this. "Maybe you should call in backup, Raven."

"We've got this," Raven answered gruffly, his pride obviously offended.

"Can I talk to Flynn? Please?"

"Uh, well, he had to um, go take a piss. I can have him call you later," Raven rambled, his former cockiness dissolving.

Malakai didn't believe him for a second. "Where is my mate?" he demanded. Panic overwhelmed him, causing his legs to shake, and he slumped down on his bed before he fell to the floor. "Is he hurt? Raven, tell me, damn it!"

"Stavion is on his way there. He'll explain everything." Then he hung up.

"Fucking coward!" Malakai screamed as he launched his phone across the room. Something was wrong. His friends and his mate were in deep shit. It was the only possible reason that Raven wouldn't tell him what was happening.

Hurrying across the room, he snatched up his phone, thankful that he hadn't demolished it. Scrolling through his recent call list, he hit the button to connect him with Stavion and waited.

"My plane just landed. I will be there in twenty minutes," his friend said by way of greeting.

"How did you know?"

"Raven sent me a text message." Stavion sighed. "I'll explain everything when I get there."

Malakai jerked his head back and frowned when the line went dead. He was getting damn tired of everyone hanging up on him. His mate was off in some godforsaken backwoods of Montana, possibly hurt, and no one would tell him what was going on.

He should call Boston. As quickly as the thought came, he dismissed it. There was no need to worry the man until he had all the facts. He trusted Stavion not to lie to him, so he just had to wait until the coven leader arrived. It was only twenty minutes. He could wait that long.

"Braxton!" Running out of his room, he sprinted down the stairs, searching for his new friends. "Keeton! Jackson!"

He'd almost made it to the kitchen when the three men came barreling out of the doorway, tripping over each other and looking panicked. "Malakai, what's wrong?" Keeton pushed past his friends and hurried over to hug him. "Did something happen?"

Clutching at Keeton's back, Malakai couldn't calm his nerves or stop the shaking of his body. "Yes. No. I don't know. Stavion is on his way here. I think something happened to Flynn."

"Calm down," Braxton said kindly as he moved over to join them in a group hug. "I'm sure Flynn is fine."

"He and Boston have claimed each other, right?" Jackson asked. When Malakai nodded, he smiled. "Then Flynn's fine. Boston would be able to feel it if something was wrong."

Okay, that made sense. Malakai sucked in a big breath of air and let it out slowly. "I guess I'm overreacting." His cheeks heated, and he dropped his head in embarrassment.

"Nope." Keeton squeezed him once more before letting him go. "He's your mate, so of course you'll worry about him. It comes with the territory, honey."

Braxton rubbed Malakai's back in comfort. "I'd love to tell you that it gets easier, but it doesn't. There's no point in making yourself sick over it until you know something, though."

"What happened?" Jackson asked, motioning for them to follow him back into the kitchen. "Why is Stavion coming here?"

Malakai shook his head as he plopped down in one of the kitchen chairs. "I don't know. I called Raven because I was worried about Flynn. He said he'd only be gone a couple of days, but it's been four. Raven said there were complications, but everyone was okay. Then I asked to talk to Flynn, and he made up some bullshit excuse about why he couldn't come to the phone. The next thing I know, he's telling me that Stavion is on his way, and then he hangs up on me."

His stomach started to roll as panic reared its ugly head again. He was just starting to get things worked out with Boston. He hadn't had nearly enough time with Flynn, but he already couldn't imagine his life without either of them. They belonged to him, and he belonged to them. They were supposed to be together forever. Why would fate throw these wonderful men in his path just to rip them away when he started getting close to them?

"Stop," Jackson said firmly. "I don't know what you're thinking, but you're shaking the whole damn table. I promise that Boston would know if something happened to Flynn."

"Yeah, okay," Malakai answered shakily. Fuck, he wished Stavion would hurry up and get there. He couldn't remember a time he'd ever been so scared. Even if Flynn wasn't hurt, there was definitely something wrong. "What if Flynn is too far away? What if Boston can't feel his pain because he's all the way across the country?"

"I honestly don't know," Jackson answered after a significant pause. "When we went to help Blaise find Willow and Cole, Blaise was scared, but he never mentioned being able to feel their emotions or their pain. When we started getting closer to where Cole was held, he and Willow both dropped like a bag of rocks from the pain." He shoved a hand through his hair and growled. "Shit, I just don't know, Malakai. I'm sorry."

It did nothing to calm him, but he was thankful that the young shifter had been honest with him. Though part shifter himself, that piece of him was so minute, he didn't exhibit any qualities of the race. He'd served as liaison between the covens and packs before, but he still didn't know a great deal about shifters. Oh, he understood most things about their day-to-day culture, but knew very little about mating bonds and other more personal matters.

They all sat in silence while Jackson moved about the kitchen, preparing them a late dinner. Malakai wasn't hungry. The smell of the spaghetti sauce bubbling on the stove just made his stomach churn. He was scared out of his mind for Flynn, pissed off that Raven had lied to him, and felt sick at the prospect of meeting with Stavion. Whatever news his friend brought, it wouldn't be good—otherwise, he would have just told Malakai over the phone.

"I could strip for you," Keeton said out of the blue. He rose gracefully from the table and started dancing around the kitchen to some nonexistent beat. "Would that make you feel better?" He smirked wickedly and reached for the top button of his jeans.

Malakai's eyes went wide and his mouth dropped open. Braxton snorted and rolled his eyes while Jackson crossed the kitchen and popped Keeton in the back of the head. "No one wants to see your skinny ass, runt."

Rubbing the back of his head, Keeton glared at Jackson. "I'm telling."

That did it. Malakai burst out laughing, clapping a hand over his mouth to muffle his amusement. Oh, these guys were too much. They reminded him so much of his friends back at the coven. Though much smaller and weaker, Keeton was so like Raven it was scary. It was never a dull moment when either of them was around.

"Thank you."

Braxton smiled and reached over to pat Malakai's hand. "We've all been there. Besides, Keeton can't help being an idiot. He was born that way."

"Hey!" Before Keeton could say more, the doorbell rang, and everyone tensed. The lighter atmosphere dissolved quickly, and Malakai was back to feeling like he was going to hurl.

"I'll get it," Braxton said quietly, rising from his chair and hurrying out of the kitchen.

Keeton slipped into the vacated seat and took Malakai's hand, giving it a light squeeze. "Whatever happens, we're all here for you, okay?"

Malakai nodded silently before his eyes snapped to Stavion when the man walked into the kitchen behind Braxton. "Tell me," Malakai croaked.

Stavion stared at him for a full minute, the muscle jumping in his jaw. When he spoke, every word was so tight it sounded like he was forcing them out through a garden hose. "How do you feel about Washington?"

"Uh, it rains a lot." Malakai felt like an idiot, but really, what was he supposed to say to that?

Stavion seemed to be eyeing Malakai's neck with great interest. "Your mates haven't claimed you?"

Shaking his head mutely, Malakai was getting more and more paranoid about where the conversation was headed. "Just spit it out, Stavion."

"I've been offered a mating contract for you from the Olympia Coven leader."

Chapter Twelve

Waking up naked and chained to a wall was not exactly how Flynn had pictured this assignment going. The last thing he remembered was sneaking away from the hotel at daylight and setting out for the three-story mansion hidden away in the woods. It was a stupid and risky move, but from the moment their plane had landed in Montana, an all-consuming rage had settled over him, driving away every thought but taking revenge on the monsters who'd hurt his mate.

He'd made it no closer than the dense forest surrounding the estate before he'd been jumped from behind. A wet cloth covered his mouth and nose, and then the world went black. Hell, he wasn't even sure how long he'd been out before waking up in the horrible basement that reeked of fear, death, and wet animal fur.

The fear and death he expected. The animal smell was new, though. He wondered how long the coven had been employing werewolves. Even in their human form, their smell was enough to make Flynn gag.

Three of them were currently approaching him in the dim light cast off by the candles in the room. With a great deal of effort, he lifted his head to meet them head-on. His wrists were manacled and chained over his head, but his feet were free, his legs sprawled out in front of him where he sat on the cold, concrete floor. It was a small thing, but it gave him hope that he'd be able to fight them off if the need arose.

He prayed they'd just come to taunt him, though. His body felt like it was made of lead, his limbs and head so heavy that he was having trouble holding his head upright. With a quiet groan, he forced his neck muscles to work until he could rest the back of his head on the cinderblocks behind him.

"You're awake."

"Aye, good of ya to notice."

His cheeky remark earned him a vicious backhand to the face. It hurt like hell, but all Flynn could think about was his mates— particularly Boston. He hoped the distance between them was great enough that his mate wouldn't feel his pain and fear. Though it wouldn't save Boston if the werewolves decided to kill Flynn, maybe he could at least keep the events leading up to his murder from affecting the man he loved.

He never imagined that he would regret claiming Boston, but he did. It had been a selfish thing to do. While he loved the younger man, he had been putting his needs before his mate's. He'd wanted so desperately to bind them together, he hadn't thought through the ramifications. Then again, he hadn't imagined that The Council would offer him this assignment when he'd sunk his teeth into Boston's neck, either.

An angry growl preluded the next smack to his face. While letting his mind drift, apparently the asshole had been talking to him. *Oops.*

"Gregory, that will be enough," a haughty voice called from across the room. The werewolves grumbled under their breaths, but stepped aside to allow a pale man dressed in bloodred robes through their ranks. "Flynn Murphy, we meet again. I was so sure I'd seen the last of you." He chuckled as though it was a very pleasant surprise. "How did you ever survive, my dear boy?"

Flynn remained quiet. He had absolutely nothing to say to the fucker.

"Oh, the silent treatment, is it?" The coven leader laughed again. "I think we can find a way to loosen your tongue." He opened his mouth to show off his pointed canines. "I do believe I am feeling up to something…vintage tonight. It has been so long since I tasted you.

I was very sorry to see you go, but am delighted that we find ourselves acquainted once more."

Lifting his robes so that he could kneel down in front of Flynn, the vampire licked his lips lecherously. Flynn felt his stomach roll, but he still couldn't move his body enough to defend himself. His temples throbbed, his mouth felt dry, and his limbs were too heavy to be of any use to him. Damn, his mates were going to kick his ass.

The mental picture of his sweet, shy little vampire handing him his ass made him chuckle. He was still laughing when the coven leader bent forward and sank his teeth into the tender flesh of his neck. His voice sounded hysterical, even to his own ears, but he couldn't stop it. He laughed and laughed as the vampire sucked greedily at his neck. He was still chuckling when his vision dimmed, and he checked out of consciousness.

* * * *

He couldn't breathe. Well, more to the point, he couldn't get enough air into his lungs. Then slender fingers wrapped around the back of his neck and forced him down so that his head rested between his knees.

"Breathe, Malakai," Braxton instructed. "Deep breaths, you can do it."

Focusing on the sound of Braxton's voice instead of the fear ricocheting around his insides, Malakai breathed deeply through his nose, and blew it out slowly through his mouth. It took a few minutes, but eventually he was able to calm his labored breathing and sit up to address Stavion.

"I'm mated. That supersedes mating contracts. You can't be serious."

"What's a mating contract?" Keeton asked in confusion. "Like an arranged marriage? Dude, that totally blows. You vamps have some seriously fucked-up ideals."

Stavion ignored him. "As your coven leader, I can deny them, but since you haven't been claimed, you're technically eligible for the contract."

Since Stavion had taken over the Redway Clan, it seemed only natural that Malakai and the other Enforcers would join the coven as well. Now, he wasn't so sure that had been a smart idea. He knew the penalty that Stavion would face if he refused Malakai's contract without good reason. "I can't let you do that."

"Well, I can't just send you off to fucking Washington!" Stavion roared.

"You have a mate who needs you," Malakai argued quietly. He was so royally fucked.

"So do you," Braxton responded just as softly. "I don't understand what's going on, but Boston and Flynn would rip the entire state apart to find you if you leave."

Malakai groaned and dropped his forehead to the kitchen table. "What if Boston claims me tonight?" He heard a phone ringing in the distance but ignored it. "Would that work?" he asked with his face still resting against the cool wood.

"No," Stavion answered sadly. "You have to be claimed by both mates. I'm sorry, Malakai. I don't know what to do."

Sitting up slowly, he scrubbed his hands over his face and sighed. "How long do I have?"

Stavion swallowed and looked away. "By dawn."

"Oh, you have got to be fucking kidding me," Braxton mumbled. "What about The Council? Can't they do something?"

"I know it seems archaic to you, but those are our laws. Any unmated vampire of age can be contracted to another coven."

"Well, I think the rules need to change," Keeton said indignantly.

"I agree, but for now, they are what they are."

"What happens if you refuse?" Jackson asked as he came back into the kitchen. Malakai hadn't even seen him leave. "You can refuse, right?"

Malakai shook his head vehemently. "No, he can't refuse. I won't let him. If he refused the contract without just cause, it would be the same as if I broke the contract once it was accepted."

"Which means?"

"Every contract has a list of certain provisions," Stavion explained. "For example, Malakai's contract states that he will be required to wear a butt plug at all times."

"What?" Braxton practically screamed.

Malakai didn't even flinch. He'd heard of his share of mating contracts, and they were all similar. Vampires in general were a kinky bunch of bastards, and most were more selfish than not. He would never be this man's mate. He would be his sex toy.

Stavion winced but continued. "If Malakai were to refuse, it would be a breach of contract, and he could be punished however his new master sees fit."

"Master?" Keeton did screech. Good grief, the man could break glass at fiftypaces. "That's not a *mating* contract, Stavion. That's fucking slavery."

"If Stavion refuses the contract without a reason, he can be punished as well," Malakai explained, ignoring Keeton's outburst. Those had been their laws long before he was born. As much as it sickened him, there was nothing he could do about it.

"I'm calling Blaise," Keeton announced, jumping to his feet and sprinting out of the room.

"Elder Winters is very fond of Willow," Braxton said with a smile. "If anyone can help, it will be them."

Stavion stiffened but didn't comment. Malakai knew it irked his friend that he couldn't do more to protect him. He could also see that Stavion was willing to get help wherever they could find it.

"If Elder Winters can buy us some time, we can get Flynn home, and everything will be fine," Braxton said after a long pause where no one else spoke.

It did little to reassure Malakai, though. He felt his panic return as he turned his gaze to Stavion once more. "Where is Flynn?"

Stavion closed his eyes and groaned. "Missing."

Before Malakai could force his heart back down his esophagus to speak, that damn annoying phone rang again. Jackson dug his cell out of his pocket, flipped it open, and pressed it to his ear. "Hey, babe. What's up?" He was silent for a long time, his face completely impassive as he listened to whatever his mate was telling him. "Right. Stavion's already here. I'll see you in a few." He paused again. "Yeah, I got it. Love you, too."

Ending the call, he slipped his phone back into his pocket and sighed. "Talon is bringing Boston home. I guess he started screaming while he was behind the bar, then just passed out. They're almost here."

Malakai started hyperventilating again. "No," he moaned brokenly. This couldn't be happening. He was supposed to live happilyeverafter with his mates. This is not how he pictured his fairytale ending.

Large hands held his face immobile, and he had to blink several times before Stavion's face came into view. "I can't lose them, Stavion. I can't."

"You're not going to. We're going to figure this out, okay? Boston will be here any minute. Look right here at me and breathe. We've been friends for a long time, and I'm not going to let you down now."

Malakai did as he was told, taking deep breaths and not taking his eyes from Stavion until he heard the front door open, and Boston called his name. Jumping out of his seat like he had springs on his ass, he flew out of the room and didn't stop running until he launched himself into Boston's arms.

His mate crushed him close, running his hands all over Malakai as though he was checking for injuries. "You're okay," Boston breathed. "You're okay." He sounded more like he was reassuring himself than trying to comfort Malakai. "I was so fucking scared."

"I'm still scared," Malakai whispered, wrapping his legs around Boston and holding him tighter. "Don't let go, okay? Just don't let go."

"It's okay, baby. I've got you. I'm right here, and I'm not going anywhere. I need you to tell me what's happening, though."

"Flynn's missing." Malakai buried his face in Boston's neck and hiccupped. "He's all alone, Boston. He needs us."

Boston's legs gave out, and if Jackson and Stavion hadn't caught him, Malakai felt sure they would have both crashed to the floor. Boston's arms never let go of him as he was eased over to the sofa and down on the cushions. "When?"

"We're not sure, but we think it was this morning while everyone was sleeping."

"Why the hell did you send him out with a bunch of vampires anyway?" Boston demanded.

"They're the best," Stavion said simply. "I was trying to keep him safe."

"Well, that didn't really fucking work, now did it?"

Malakai whimpered, pressing closer to Boston's chest. "Please don't fight." His brain couldn't take anymore. He was still rebelling against the idea that one of his mates was missing, and he was to be sold off like a cheap set of china.

"There's something else."

"No." Malakai shook his head hard, willing Stavion to keep his big, stupid mouth shut. He'd have to tell Boston, but they needed to figure out how to help Flynn before he threw his problems into the mix.

But, of course, Stavion completely ignored him as he outlined the issues with the mating contract he'd received for Malakai. And, just as Malakai knew he would, Boston flew off the damn handle. He never released his hold on Malakai, but his chest vibrated as he growled, snarled, and called Stavion every name in the book.

"Mine!" he finished his rant with a possessive growl.

Then Malakai's head was jerked back by his hair and sharp canines pierced the side of his neck. "Boston!" Malakai screamed as he felt the mating bond snap into place. His dick swelled instantly, cum erupting from the slit before it was even fully hard.

Boston released him, licking over the mark on his neck and causing Malakai to shiver. "My turn, little one. Claim me as yours."

He didn't have to be told twice. Rocking his hips and grinding his still hard cock against Boston's midsection, Malakai sank his fangs into the salty flesh at the apex of Boston's neck and sighed when he felt the last piece fall into place. Boston was his. For better or for worse, the man would always be his.

Extracting his fangs, he licked the bite closed and sat up to look into his mate's eyes. They stared at each other for a long time before Boston crushed their lips together and attacked Malakai's mouth like a starving man. "Not letting you go, baby. You're mine," he panted when they finally came up for air. "We're going to get Flynn back, and no one is ever going to take you from us. Okay? Do you trust me to take care of you?"

Malakai nodded mutely. He trusted Boston with his life.

"Then don't worry about this stupid contract. It's bullshit. I will gut anyone that tries to take you away. Got it? You belong here." He patted Malakai on the hip and urged him off his lap. "Go take a shower and decompress, baby. I'll be up in a minute to take care of you."

Bobbing his head again when he couldn't form words, Malakai made his way up the stairs and down the hall to the bathroom. He was still scared for Flynn, still worried about this coven from Washington, but Boston said he would make everything right.

He wouldn't be fighting alone, though. Malakai would do whatever it took to protect his men. Holding that conviction close to his heart, he climbed into the shower and let the warm water wash away the last of his doubts.

* * * *

Flynn wanted to die. He was fairly certain he was going to get his wish, too. The coven leader had drank from him twice, and then brought his inner circle—three large and burly vampires—to feed from him as well.

He didn't know how much time had passed, or how many times he'd passed out. He imagined it was close to nightfall on his second day inside the basement. There had been an extended gap between the vampires' visits, which most likely meant they'd been sleeping.

It didn't matter. Either they would drain him dry and dump him out in the forest to rot, or he'd become their pet again. When he'd found himself free after his last stint in the basement, he swore he'd never go back.

First came the feedings, next was the mind control and manipulation. Then when they'd used his body and depleted his veins of blood, he'd be cast aside just as before. He'd rather skip the in between and just get right on to the dead part.

How could he do that to his mates, though? By claiming Boston, the man's life would be forfeit as well when Flynn took his last breath. He knew Boston would understand, would mostly likely feel the same way if their places were reversed, but where did that leave Malakai?

So the war raged on. Find a way to end his misery and take Boston with him, leaving Malakai to a lonely existence. Or find a way to fight and get back to his men.

"Oh, look, he's awake," a growly voice taunted.

Flynn rolled his head to the side and blinked. That little bit of movement sent pain coursing through his body, and he gritted his teeth to keep from groaning.

"Maybe he wants to play," another voice sang. A large werewolf knelt in front of him, his stench enough to make Flynn's stomach convulse and bile rise up in his throat. "You want to play with the big boys little shifter?"

Flynn wished he could do more than just stare stupidly at the asshole. His body wouldn't function, though. "Go away," he slurred. He wasn't afraid of the weres. He didn't even care if they used him as a punching bag, but he did fear Boston could feel his pain. When the coven leader had first bitten him, just before he'd checked out, he'd felt a tinge of fear, just on the outside of his subconscious, and he was pretty sure it hadn't been his. Whatever happened, he wanted to save Boston from as much of his suffering as he could.

"You heard what the boss man said," the first werewolf responded, and he sounded disappointed about it. "We're not to touch him. He belongs to the head bloodsucker."

The guy crouched in front of Flynn growled and shoved to his feet. "Yeah, yeah. Let's go find one we can play with."

As the werewolves sauntered away, Flynn felt his chest swell, his heart pound, and something shifted inside him. His skin tingled, his shoulder throbbed where Boston's claiming bite was located, and once again he felt the mating bond snap into place.

It wasn't his, though. It was Boston and Malakai. He didn't know what had happened since he'd been gone, but his mates had finally found their way together and claimed one another. His joy at the realization lasted only seconds before the gravity of the situation hit him like a battering ram.

The likelihood that he would make it out alive was slim to none. Now that Boston had claimed Malakai, their life forces would be bonded, just as his and Boston's were. If Flynn died, Boston died. When Boston died, Malakai died.

So in essence, he was killing his mates. Maybe they'd all be together in the next life. He doubted it. He'd already been given a second chance, and he'd let his need for revenge lead him into disaster, causing him to screw that up, too. Hell, he didn't even deserve another chance.

No! He was not going to give up. He'd fought too bloody hard to waste the gift fate had given him. He had men counting on him. Men who cared for him, trusted him, and needed him. Their very lives depended on Flynn's strength and perseverance.

With a new resolve, he closed his eyes, letting thoughts of his mates fuel his determination to find a way back to them.

Chapter Thirteen

He did it. He'd claimed Malakai as his own. The overwhelming sense of protectiveness that welled up inside of him as he'd felt their hearts, souls, and minds intertwine was indescribable. Flynn and Malakai were his, and Boston would die before he let anyone take them from him.

"You find a way to make this right." Rising to his feet, he stood toe-to-toe with Stavion, leaning so close to him that their noses almost touched. "I don't give a shit if the gods themselves want Malakai. He's mine."

"I don't want to do this," Stavion answered calmly. "Unless Flynn claims him as well, my hands are tied. I have a mate, too, Boston. I know what you're feeling."

"You," Boston snarled, "have no idea what I'm feeling. It took me a long motherfuckin' time to pull my head out of my ass. I've been alone for eight years. Count them, Stavion, eight goddamn years. Those vampires took something from me that I can never get back, but I have Flynn and Malakai now. My mates are the *only* thing I care about—not your messed up laws."

"Boston, I'm doing everything I can." Stavion still spoke quietly, still stood his ground, not flinching away from the cold steel in Boston's voice.

Maybe he wasn't getting his point across if the man could stare back at him so calmly. He couldn't get those eight years back that he'd lost with Flynn. He couldn't take back the things he'd said and done to Malakai when they'd first met. All he could do was make sure that he never wasted a single moment with them, never took for granted the second chance he'd been given.

"Boston, man, calm down." Talon's hand landed on his shoulder and tugged him back from the vampire. "You know we're on your side. We're going to do whatever it takes to make sure you keep your mates."

Shrugging off Talon's hold on him, Boston marched over to the stairs, but paused with his foot on the first step. "If you're really Malakai's friend," he said without turning around, "then you'll help him. If you ever cared anything about him, you won't let this happen." Then he jogged up the staircase and all the way to Malakai's room. Slipping inside, his heart broke at the lost look on his mate's face.

Malakai sat completely nude on the edge of the bed and stared straight ahead. His dark hair was still damp from his shower, and beads of water clung to his pale skin. He didn't acknowledge Boston's entrance, didn't even twitch when Boston eased down on the mattress beside him.

"Baby, look at me."

"You were so angry," Malakai whispered. "I could feel it. I think I broke the shower."

"We'll fix it." Boston gathered Malakai into his arms and rocked his slowly. "Yeah, I was angry, but not at you. Everything is going to be okay."

He felt himself melt when Malakai curled into his chest and nuzzled against him. "I know. I'm not worried. I decided something while you were downstairs."

Boston grinned into Malakai's hair. He could feel the peace and contentment rolling off his mate, and it made him feel like a king that his mate felt so safe with him. Yeah, he'd done a lot of things wrong where his men were concerned, but he'd spend the rest of his life making it right. "What did you decide, baby?"

"That fate wouldn't have thrown us together if we didn't fit. We all have darkness in our pasts, but maybe that's why we're perfect together. Maybe we're supposed to heal each other."

"I think you're right," Boston whispered. He eased Malakai down to the mattress before standing and stripping out of his clothes. He grimaced at his sticky groin, using his boxers to wipe away the remnants of his earlier climax in the living room.

Then he crawled into bed beside his mate, getting them situated under the blankets, and spooned around his baby. "Thank you for not giving up on me."

"I could say the same thing." Malakai turned over and cuddled closer until their chests pressed together. "Can I ask how you met Flynn?"

Resting his chin on the top of Malakai's head, he held the man tightly as he thought back. "I was a late bloomer, I guess you could say. I didn't shift for the first time until I was sixteen. Well, I'm sure you know about the curse. I thought my mom was going to have a heart attack."

"Because you're a Moonlighter?"

Boston nodded. "Hell, it might have happened without that, but me being a white shifter finally gave them the excuse they needed to get rid of me. No one wanted to risk going insane if I happened to shift around them."

Malakai leaned away far enough to look up in Boston's eyes and frowned. "Blaise says that you guys aren't dangerous like everyone thought."

"Xander told me." Boston smiled a little and kissed the tip of his mate's nose. "Just because our magic only effects people that piss us off when we shift, it's not going to change anything, baby. We're still going to be feared. We're still going to be hunted."

Malakai sighed in resignation as he cuddled back against Boston's chest. "I guess you're right, but that doesn't mean I have to like it."

Boston chuckled, thrilled to his toes with his lover's indignation on his behalf.

"Okay, so what happened? How did you end up with the coven in Montana?"

Boston nuzzled Malakai's hair, letting his mate's scent calm him and give him courage to continue. "Well, of course, everyone was afraid of me, and their solution was to sell me to a nearby vampire coven. They needed the money, and they needed rid of me, so it was a no-brainer."

"Your parents didn't stop them? Why do you think they would have sold you regardless?"

Boston chuckled at Malakai's huffy tone. It was nice to have someone on his side for a change. "No, sweetheart. I was never really close with my parents, and they got the biggest cut of the money. It was stupid easy for them to get rid of me."

"Oh, babe, I'm so sorry." Malakai stroked his chest lovingly. "So, you met Flynn when you went to the coven?"

"I was there for about four months before they brought him in." Boston still remembered how his heart had kicked against his sternum when he'd scented the man. Who the hell was ever lucky enough to find their mate at sixteen? "He was so gorgeous, even all battered and bruised. I knew immediately that he was my mate."

"That's kind of romantic." Malakai sniffled. "Even after all you'd been through, you were able to find your mate in that awful place."

Boston stroked his mate's hair and smiled. "Oh, it was far from romantic. Flynn is three years older than me. It was a full two years before I finally talked him into making love to me."

"He's a noble man. You can't fault him for that."

Boston's grin stretched wider as he thought back to all the times he practically begged Flynn to take him. The man was stubborn beyond reason, refusing to "impugn" Boston's honor until he'd become of age. "No, I don't guess I can." The smile slid from his face, and he shuddered. "Our first time was with seven vampires watching us."

"That's awful," Malakai gasped, pushing up on his elbow to look into Boston's eyes. "No wonder you hated me so much."

"I didn't hate you, baby." He palmed Malakai's cheek and ran the pad of his thumb over the man's lips. "You just scared the shit out of me. I always thought I would die in the basement. That's why I never let Flynn claim me. I couldn't let anything happen to him."

"Did the coven know you were mates?"

"I don't think so. Flynn wasn't sold like me. They captured him when he was out running one night."

Malakai's nose scrunched and his eyebrows drew together. "I thought Flynn was from Ireland?"

"Originally, yes. He moved to the states about a year before he was captured. I'm not sure if he intended to make this his final stop, but he was young and restless and wanted to see the world." Boston chuckled softly. "He's amazing."

"You love him so much." Malakai didn't sound hurt or jealous. In fact, he sounded peaceful.

"I do. I care about you Malakai. I'm not sure that it's love, but I know that I would do anything to keep you safe."

Malakai kissed his lips and smiled sweetly. "You barely know me, Boston. I don't expect you to love me. As long as you think you might one day, that's enough for me."

"Oh, yeah, I can definitely see myself falling hard for you, baby. Just keep being you and give me a little more time. I have no doubt that you're going to wiggle your way right into my heart."

His mate kissed him again. "I can live with that." When he pulled away his eyes shimmered with unshed tears. "He's hurt really bad isn't he? That's why you passed out and Talon had to bring you home. You felt it."

Boston didn't want to scare Malakai, but he didn't want to lie to him either. "Yeah, he's hurt, but Flynn is the toughest son of a bitch I know. We're going to find him, and he's going to be okay."

"I trust you, Boston."

"Thank you. Just don't use your freaky mind control stuff on me, okay? That shit wigs me out." He hadn't meant to be quite so blunt about it, but Malakai needed to know everything. "The vampires used to love to torture us by slipping into our heads and planting these gruesome pictures. Or they'd manipulate us into doing things like stripping off our clothes, or jacking off for their enjoyment."

Malakai looked sick by the time Boston had finished speaking. "I would never do that to you, Boston. I swear it. I haven't used it on you, and I never will."

"I believe you, baby. I just wanted you to know." Deciding he was done with conversation, he rolled Malakai to his back and insinuated himself between his mate's thighs. "I want you," he murmured against the silky smooth skin of Malakai's throat. "Please, say yes."

Malakai moaned, dropping his head back to give Boston more room to play. "Yes," he hissed.

As he licked and kissed over Malakai's flushed skin, Boston's cock swelled between them,and he ground his hips against Malakai's,groaning when their heated erections slid together. "I'm going to make you feel so good."

Whimpering and writhing beneath him, Malakai's hands gripped at his shoulders and his small body trembled beautifully. "Please," he begged.

Oh, Boston liked begging. His dick flexed, throbbing almost painfully and reminding him that he'd have time for slow teasing later. Just then, he needed inside his mate before he lost his fucking mind. "Please tell me you have lube."

"Don't need it," Malakai panted.

"Baby, I'm not going to hurt you. I need to stretch you, and I need something to ease the way."

"Don't need it," Malakai repeated, arching up against Boston and looping his legs around Boston's hips. "I hope you don't think I'm presumptuous, but you did promise to make love to me tonight." He took Boston's hand and glided it down his body, right to his well-stretched hole. "I wanted to be ready for you, so I used a butt plug. I took it out when I came back to the room and applied more lube."

Boston didn't know whether to growl or whimper. It was totally Malakai, though—so very practical and considerate. Pushing two fingers into his lover's velvety heat, Boston pumped the digits a few times to make sure Malakai was stretched well enough to take him. Confident that he wouldn't hurt his mate, he extracted his fingers and lined his cock up with Malakai's slippery hole.

He sank in slowly, gritting his teeth to keep from ramming home in one mighty plunge. Damn, Malakai felt like heaven, like home. By the time he'd bottomed out and his heavy sac brushed against Malakai's pert ass, sweat was pouring off him in rivers. "You are so damn tight," he groaned.

"It's been a while." Malakai moaned and clamped his muscles down around Boston's pulsing cock. "Move."

"Damn, ease up, baby." Malakai's ass held a stranglehold on his cock, and it was all Boston could do to not blow his load then and there.

Malakai's muscles relaxed enough for Boston to begin a slow, gentle glide. "I adore that you thought of me and wanted to make our first time as easy as possible." He petted Malakai's hair back from his face as he kept his movements lazy and tender. "You are not a whore or my plaything, though. I like stretching you and giving you pleasure. It makes me feel good to know that I can make you fly."

Malakai stared up at him for a long time before a wicked smile spread over his face. "Then make me fly, big guy."

Growling playfully, Boston nipped at Malakai's neck in reprimand as he increased his pace, rocking into him with enough force to move them up the bed. "You are mine. Me and Flynn are the only ones who will ever make you fly. Say it, Malakai. Tell me who you belong to." His playful mood slipped away to be replaced by a clawing need to dominate his smaller mate. "Say it!" He punctuated his demand with a hard jab, tilting the smaller man's hips up and nailing his prostate.

"You!" Malakai screamed, the cords in his neck flexing as his eyes rolled back in his head. "Only you and Flynn. I swear."

"Perfect." Satisfied with his lover's response, Boston let his control go and slammed into his mate's welcoming body with abandon. He never wanted to stop, but apparently, his body had other ideas. Electricity raced up his spine and his belly tightened, heralding his impending climax.

Reaching between their sweat soaked bodies, he fisted Malakai's rigid cock and stroked him hard and fast with every thrust of his hips. "Come for me, baby. You belong to me, and I want you to come for me."

Screaming out Boston's name, Malakai's body went stiff beneath him as pearly ropes of cream spurted from his slit to slash against his belly. The sight of Malakai's face, the scent of his seed, the way his inner walls convulsed around his cock and milked it, sent Boston careening over the edge and into orgasmic bliss.

Burying his face in Malakai's throat, he groaned long and low as his movements stilled and he pumped his seed into his mate's heated depths, further claiming the man as his own. Sex with Flynn was intense. Sex with Malakai was mind-blowing. If they could ever get their shit together, and Boston could get them both in his bed, he imagined he might just die from the pleasure.

"Amazing," he breathed, giving Malakai's neck a soft kiss. "You are amazing."

He started to become worried when he didn't receive a response. Had Malakai not enjoyed it? Had he hurt his lover? Pushing up on his arms to look into Malakai's face, Boston couldn't help the cocky grin that spread over his face.

Malakai was passed out cold. And if that didn't make him feel like a sex god, he didn't know what could. Slipping gently from Malakai's still-twitching hole, he hurried out of the room and down the hall to the bathroom.

Washing himself quickly, he grabbed another wet cloth and raced back to the room to attend to his mate. Malakai was still asleep, and bless his heart, he didn't even move as Boston cleaned him.

Once he had all his mate's bits and pieces cleansed, Boston tossed the cloth toward the door, climbed in bed with Malakai, and cuddled him close. Wherever Flynn was, whatever was happening to him, he hoped the man knew that he wasn't alone and that help was coming.

He allowed himself just another few minutes to soak up Malakai's warmth, then kissed his baby's temple before slipping away and pulling on his jeans—sans the sticky underwear. He didn't want Malakai to wake up alone, especially after what they'd just shared, but he needed to talk to Stavion and figure out a plan to not only rescue Flynn, but keep Malakai safe as well.

Taking one last look at the peaceful look on Malakai's angelic face, Boston left the room and went in search of answers.

Chapter Fourteen

Coming awake for the umpteenth time since he'd been kidnapped, Flynn blinked to dispel the bleariness, but nothing worked. He felt light-headed, and his body seemed weighted down. The slow, sluggish pulse of his heart scared him the most, but he didn't even have the strength left to panic.

He had a new strength, though, a reason to fight. Flynn couldn't have been prouder of Boston for overcoming his fears and uncertainties and claiming Malakai as his own. He hoped to have the chance to claim the little vampire as well. He'd felt it again when they'd made love, the deep contentment and rising protectiveness that bubbled inside of Boston.

When his men had come together in the night, deepening their bond, it had felt like sunshine bursting in his soul. He wanted that connection with Malakai as well. They were meant to be together—all three of them—and Flynn would see it happen by any means necessary.

The deep sense of *rightness*that filled him made his eyes sting and his throat burn. Maybe he didn't know the tiny vampire that well, but that didn't stop Flynn from needing him. Call him a sentimental fool, but he'd always believed in love at first sight, and that there was one special person—or in this case, two people—that fate had designed just for him. Hey, he was Irish after all, a romantic by nature. He also believed in miracles, and prayed whoever made the rules had a special one they were saving just for him.

"Flynn, I hate you," came a rough voice to his side.

With a lot of effort, he managed to turn his head to find a shadowy figure sitting beside him. He couldn't get his eyes to focus well enough to make out a face, but he thought he recognized the voice. "Raven?"

"Yeah, it's me, asshole."

"And fine day to ya as well." Maybe he was hallucinating. It was the only explanation for Raven's sudden appearance. "I'm dyin'."

"Well, tough. We're getting you out of here, so you're going to have to postpone that for a while."

"Daylight," Flynn mumbled. His tongue felt too big for his mouth, and every word ripped at his aching throat.

"Not yet, but close. It's almost dawn, so we need to hurry."

The man was going to get himself fried. "Werewolves."

"Yeah, I know. The boys have the guards tied up out back. We gotta get you out of here, though. Can you move at all?"

Flynn nodded carefully, but stopped when he felt like he was being stabbed in the temple with a rusted knife.

"Okay, then let's get out of here." Raven slipped an arm around Flynn's waist and hoisted him to his feet with a grunt.

It was only then that Flynn noticed his wrists were no longer chained to the wall. Damn, what else had he missed? Deciding to worry about it later, he focused all of his energy on just putting one foot in front of the other.

"Fuck, we have to move faster, Flynn. I'm really sorry about this." Then the Enforcer spun around, dipping his shoulder into Flynn's midsection and swinging him up in a fireman's carry. "You can kick my ass later, but we have to get out of here."

Flynn didn't give a shit how they got out of there as long as they made it out alive. If that meant that he had to swallow his pride and let Raven carry him, then so be it. He had people back home counting on him, and neither Boston nor Malakai gave a rat's ass that he was supposed to be the alpha in their relationship. The thought make him snicker. Oh, his loves were going to be pissed at him.

He must have blacked out after that, because the next time he opened his eyes, he found himself in the back of a speeding SUV. "We have to get out of the sun," Raven was explaining to him. "We'll get you home soon, though. I know Malakai is anxious to see you."

*Miracles.*Flynn smiled just a little, thanking that unknown deity. Then he passed out again.

* * * *

"Baby, you need to be in bed. The sky is already starting to lighten."

"I'll be fine for a little longer," Malakai assured his mate, though he felt exhausted to his toes. "I want to help."

He'd woken cold and alone and hadn't liked it one bit. After dressing quickly, he'd hurried down the stairs to find Boston doing his whole growly thing at Stavion. The coven leader was taking the abuse, but Malakai could see right through his friend's calm façade. Stepping in before the men started trading punches, he'd gotten them separated, and then the real fun had begun.

While Blaise had managed to buy them some time from The Council, Elder Winters could only postpone the mating contract for an additional twenty-four hours. That gave them until midnight to find Flynn, get him home, and convince him to claim Malakai. *Piece of cake.*

They'd argued back and forth all night about ways to get inside the coven estate and rescue Flynn without being captured themselves. Because, of course, that would help no one if they ended up in the basement right beside Flynn.

Raven, being the ray of sunshine that he was, had reported that the coven had werewolves guarding the place during the day. How he knew that, Malakai didn't know, but ewww, gross. Werewolves were the most disgusting creatures he'd ever met. Vile and repulsive, he wondered exactly what the vampires of Montana were trading for the guard detail.

"I'm taking you to bed," Boston announced in a no-nonsense tone. "You are dead on your feet."

"I'm sitting down."

"Don't be a smartass. You know what I meant." Boston scooped him up and rubbed their cheeks together. "You're pale and look like a gentle breeze could knock you over. You need to feed, and then you need to sleep."

"What about Flynn?" Malakai wanted to scream in frustration. How was he supposed to sleep when he knew his mate was being tortured? Now that Boston had claimed him and they were linked, he'd felt it all. He might not be able to feel Flynn directly, but he'd felt the man's pain through Boston. How could he possibly ignore that just to sleep?

"I've got Blaise working on it. He says two favors in one day is going to cost me big." Boston chuckled as he started walking. "I don't care as long as he finds Flynn."

"So, he's sending backup?" Malakai sagged in Boston's arms, so relieved, he thought he'd pass out from it.

"Yeah, baby. I'm not a warrior, and I know that. As much as I'd love to rush in and play the white knight, I'd just end up doing more damage. Blaise has never let us down."

Malakai almost jumped out of his skin when Stavion's cell phone began ringing. "Wait," he hissed at his mate, eager to find out who was on the other end of the line.

"Right. Okay. Tomorrow, it has to be tomorrow. I'm glad you're okay, man. Yeah, I'll talk to you later." Stavion snapped his phone closed and shoved it into his pocket as his lips split into a wide grin. "That was Raven. They've got Flynn.He's sleeping right now, but he will be here as soon as the sun goes down."

"Thank you," Malakai whispered to his friend, his voice filled with emotion. Then he squeezed Boston tight and attacked his mouth with so much enthusiasm, the shifter lost his balance, and they both tumbled to the floor, laughing like idiots. "He's coming home!"

"I told you so," Boston teased. "Now, it's time for all good little vampires to be in bed." He kissed Malakai on the lips and turned his attention to Stavion. "And big vampires. You can take Malakai's room. I'll swipe the blackout curtains from Xander's room for the day."

"Uh, babe, Stavion is a full-blood vampire. He can't be in any light." He could already see that his friend was in pain just from the dim light filtering in through the blinds. "Is there anywhere else? Do you have a basement?"

"Nope." Boston looked up at Stavion again. "I have a walk-in closet, man. That's the best I can do. I'm sorry."

Stavion waved him away. "I appreciate it. Not to be a pain in the ass, but I need to go like five minutes ago."

Malakai jumped to his feet and motioned Stavion to follow him. Once he had the man settled in the closet—how ironic was that? A gay vampire in the closet—he crept back to his room, careful not to wake the other residents of the household.

"Come sleep, baby." Boston sounded as exhausted as Malakai felt. He lifted one side of the sheets and patted the mattress beside him. "Get your sexy ass over here."

Stripping out of his clothes, Malakai dove onto the bed and wound himself around his mate. "Do you think Flynn will claim me?"

"Yes," Boston said around a huge yawn. "Do you need to feed before you go to sleep?"

"Nope, I'm good until we wake up. Do you really think he'll want to keep me?" If Flynn decided he wasn't worth it, he was going to be so screwed. He wouldn't force the man into it, though, wouldn't guilt him or manipulate him, either.

"Yes, now shut up and go to sleep."

Smiling to himself, Malakai curled closer to his grumpy lover and closed his eyes.

* * * *

Boston was standing on the front porch, holding Malakai's hand when the SUV came to a stop in front of their house. Malakai was practically vibrating where he stood, shifting from foot to foot in his eagerness to see their mate.

When Flynn stepped out of the passenger side door and smiled at them, Boston finally took his first real breath since the man had left. Flynn looked pale and tired, but otherwise unharmed. It took everything he had not to throw himself off the porch and tackle the man to the gravel. Knowing that Malakai needed this more than him, though, he released his lover's hand and gave him a little nudge. "Go get him, baby."

Malakai didn't hesitate. He hurdled the porch steps, flew across the short distance, and jumped into Flynn's waiting arms. Watching Flynn catch their mate and whirl him around, Boston smiled to himself as he made his way down the steps and out to join his men.

"Welcome home," he whispered when he reached them.

Still clutching Malakai in one arm, Flynn wound his fingers around the back of Boston's neck and dragged him into a fiercely possessive kiss. "Missed you, *a ghrá.*" He rested their foreheads together, closed his eyes, and just breathed.

"Let's get you inside," Boston said after a moment of basking in his lover's affection. "We need to talk."

"Oh, are ya leavin' me for the wee vamp then?" Flynn asked. His voice was light and teasing, and Boston didn't feel any uncertainty flowing off the man, so he just smiled and shook his head.

"It's my fault," Malakai murmured, still clinging to Flynn like a spider monkey. "Don't be mad, okay?"

"I'll not be mad, little one. Just tell me what it is that has ya worried."

"Let's get you some dinner," Boston suggested. "You look like you're about to fall over." He reached for Malakai, but Flynn wouldn't let go.

"I'll be carryin' him," Flynn said firmly. His other arm wound around Boston's waist,and he led them toward the front door.

Rolling his eyes, Boston let his lover take charge. Even after everything he'd been through, Flynn still had to play the alpha instead of just allowing them to take care of him. Or maybe it was *because* of the things he'd been through. Perhaps his big Irishman just needed to take back some control.

Whatever the reason, Boston decided to go with it. As long as it made Flynn happy, he wouldn't complain. Smiling at Raven as they passed him, he motioned for the man to join them inside. He couldn't begin to repay the Enforcer for bringing Flynn back to them, but he'd spend the rest of his life trying to at least make a dent in the debt that he owed.

"Now tell me what needs tellin'," Flynn said when they reached the kitchen. Boston helped him into one of the chairs, chuckling when the man still refused to give up his hold on Malakai.

Flynn dragged another chair close to him, and patted the seat for Boston to sit. Rolling his eyes, Boston gave in, sitting as close to his lover as he could get without crawling up in Flynn's lap along with Malakai. Judging by the look on Flynn's face, that's exactly where he wanted Boston, but it so wasn't happening.

"I'm close enough right here, Flynn."

Flynn just grunted, wrapped his arms around Boston's shoulders, and tucked him into his side. While Boston understood Flynn's need to keep them close and assure himself that he and Malakai were safe and well, the behavior could become old really fast.

"Hey!" Boston rubbed the back of his head, glaring at Malakai. "What the fuck was that for?"

"Stop being annoyed. I think it's sweet that he wants to hold us. You're ruining it for me."

His eyes nearly bugged out of his head at the reprimand. His sweet, passive little vampire was chastising him?

"You're doing it again," Malakai mumbled, skimming his nose along Flynn's throat. "Shut up and let me enjoy this."

Boston snorted, leaned up to kiss both of his mates, then stood to go find them something to eat. "Malakai, I know you're thirsty, but you can't drink from Flynn just yet."

"I'm not stupid, Boston." Malakai's tone implied that he'd have a few choice words for Boston later. Boston imagined he probably deserved them.

"Would ya two stop ya bickerin' and tell me what I'm needin' to know?"

Boston set about making omelets—sans meat for him and Flynn—as he rehashed what Stavion had told them about the mating contract from the Olympia Coven. He had to stop twice and clear his throat to get his mates' attention when they started sucking at each other's mouths.

He finished the story at the same time he finished their dinner, and carried the plates to the table. "So, I know it's kind of sudden and all, but the only way to get Malakai out of this contract is for both of us to claim him before midnight." Boston glanced over his shoulder to see the clock on the microwave. "And, it looks like you have about forty-five minutes to make your decis—"

"Flynn!"

Boston whipped back around just in time to see Malakai shudder in Flynn's arms as the shifter licked over his mating bite on the little man's neck. Boston snorted. "Never mind."

Chapter Fifteen

Flynn ate in silence, feeling better than he had in years. With the blood Raven had given him after his rescue, and the small infusion of Malakai's blood when he claimed him, he was already beginning to heal, and all he could think about was getting his mates up to their room and ravishing them both until none of them could walk for days.

Still, there were questions he needed answered before he whisked them off to fulfill all his carnal fantasies. "So, this vampire that's wantin' ya?"

"I met him once," Malakai answered, catching his train of thought. "It was right before the whole mess happened in Wyoming. I honestly didn't say more than a handful of sentences to the man. I have no idea why he wants me."

Flynn grunted and continued eating. While his claiming bite had nullified the contract, he doubted this vampire from Washington would give up easily. Men in power never could accept no for an answer.

"What?" Boston asked. "Do you think we're going to have trouble with him?"

"Aye, I do. I'm thinkin' he'll not be swayed from what he's wantin'."

"The contract is void now," Malakai said with confidence. "There's nothing he can do about it."

Oh, look at his little vampire getting all indignant. "Not to worry, my darlin'. He'll not be havin' ya."

"Damn right, he won't." Malakai huffed and stabbed angrily at his eggs. "I'm right where I belong, and he can just go fuck himself."

Flynn chuckled softly as his heart pounded inside his chest. Malakai's fierceness, and his conviction that he belonged with them, made Flynn want to purr with satisfaction. It also made his dick throb inside his jeans. "Are ya done then?" He pointed to Malakai's plate.

"Uh, I guess so. Why?"

Instead of giving a verbal answer, Flynn stood from his chair, grabbed Malakai, and flung him over his shoulder, swatting his ass when the man struggled against him. A soft moan fell from Malakai's lips, and he went limp, sagging over Flynn's shoulder. Flynn liked that a lot, and he planned to exploit his lover's hidden kink to his advantage.

"Well, are ya comin'?" he asked Boston. "Or will ya be sittin' this one out?"

Boston was out of his chair and stripping off his clothes before Flynn even had the words out of his mouth. Delighted with his lover's eagerness, he spanked Boston on his gorgeous ass, hustling him out of the room and toward the stairs.

They didn't make it any farther than the carpeted space behind the sofa, though, before Boston was on him, lifting Malakai out of his arms and depositing him on his feet. The feral glint in his mates' eyes had Flynn swallowing hard and praying that he didn't embarrass himself by coming in his jeans.

They didn't just jump him, they attacked him, pulling him to the floor and ripping his clothes off, shredding his shirt and tearing his pants. When they had him naked, the primal grunts and animalistic growls of approval went straight to Flynn's cock, making it flex against his lower belly as he sprawled on his back, completely at his men's mercy.

Malakai crawled up his chest, straddling his hips, and moaning when their swollen cocks rubbed together. "Missed you," Malakai groaned before slanting his mouth over Flynn's and pillaging the warm depths of his mouth.

Oh, Lord, the man consumed him, inhaled him, and completely devoured him. The soft snick of a bottle cap drew his attention, but he wouldn't give up his claim to Malakai's mouth to investigate further. He didn't know where the lube had come from, but he didn't really question it. He couldn't even count the tubes of KY and Astroglide he'd found stashed in every imaginable place around the house. With three sets of horny mates on the premises, he supposed it was only to be expected.

Malakai stiffened above him, moaning into his mouth, before his muscles relaxed, and he started rocking his groin against Flynn's. "Yes, please. Yes, please," he chanted, and the sound was so beautiful, Flynn's cock swelled further and leaked against his abs.

Gripping Malakai's hips in a bruising hold, he thrust up against his lover, grinding their dicks together.

"Almost," Boston panted. "One more finger."

He must have chosen that moment to insert that finger, because Malakai's head fell back on his shoulders, and he cried out to the ceiling. Oh, sweet hell, was there anything more amazing than the sights and sounds of his men's desires? If there was, Flynn had yet to witness it.

"Hurry, Boston. I'm needin' to feel this sweet little arse wrapped around my cock."

"Patience," Boston threw his words from their first time back at him. Flynn could even hear the smirk in his lover's voice.

He thought about arguing, but then those warm, slippery fingers turned their attention on his clenching pucker, and all thoughts fled. A deep growl rumbled in his chest, and his eyes rolled back in his head as Boston pumped two thick fingers into his needy hole.

"You have a gorgeous ass, baby," Boston crooned. "It's going to look so pretty wrapped around my cock. Gonna make you scream, Flynn."

Malakai sat up to look into Flynn's eyes, smiling mischievously. "Are you going to scream for us, Flynn? Are you going to come in my tight ass and mark me from the inside out?"

"Sweet Jesus." Flynn moaned, dropping his head back to the carpet and arching his hips up when Boston inserted a third finger. The burn was minor, the pleasure overwhelming any discomfort almost immediately.

"Are you ready for me, love?"

Flynn grunted his agreement, rocking his hips back against Boston's hand. Those long fingers slipped out of his ass, replaced by the blunt tip of Boston's cock. "Tell me if it hurts, and I'll stop."

"Don't stop," Flynn begged when Boston began pushing into his ass. He wasn't a virgin by any means, but it had been a long time since anyone had taken his ass. "So good."

Inch by torturous inch, Boston fed his monster cock to Flynn's channel, groaning when he finally bottomed out and his balls nestled against Flynn's ass. He held still, seemingly to give Flynn a chance to adjust to his thick girth. Then he patted Malakai's hip, urging him up. "Climb on, baby. This isn't going to last long."

Malakai wiggled forward until Flynn's hard length slid along the crease of his firm bottom. Cool liquid dribbled down Flynn's cock and over his balls. "Hold on, cowboy," Malakai teased then lifted his hips up, positioning the weeping tip of Flynn's crown against his slick hole.

Taking a deep breath and letting it out slowly, Malakai dropped down in one quick movement, impaling himself on Flynn's cock until his soft butt cheeks rubbed against the top of Flynn's thighs.

"*A ghrá!*" Flynn's grasp tightened on Malakai's waist, holding on for dear life as the man rode him hard and fast.

The tight, wet heat surrounding his throbbing shaft made his head spin, his balls churn, and his own ass clench greedily around the invading length inside his dark depths. His knees were pushed to the sides and back toward his chest, opening him wider as Boston began an all-out assault, pounding into his body at a demanding tempo. He could feel every ridge and vein, each pulse of Boston's heart against his inner walls.

Malakai planted his hands on Flynn's chest, his face the most exquisite mixture of pleasure and pain as he jackhammered his hips, pushing Flynn closer to the edge with every plunge. Boston's rhythm slowed, his hips rolling in waves that did deliciously sinful things to Flynn's body.

"Close," Boston grunted.

Malakai moaned his agreement as he bent forward, scraping his canines along the column of Flynn's throat, then licking away the sting. "I want you to scream now, Flynn. I want you to come in my ass and scream so loud that you shake the windows. You are mine." Then he punctuated the statement by sinking his canines into Flynn's shoulder.

Flynn felt the last piece of the mating bond snap into place, coursing through his blood like fire and setting his nerve endings sizzling. Boston looped his arms around Flynn's thighs and jerked him back as he slammed forward and pegged Flynn's sweet spot.

The pleasure was too much, too intense, and Flynn didn't fall, he hurdled over the edge, screaming until his throat felt raw and pumping his semen into Malakai's convulsing hole. Warm, sticky cum shot from Malakai's slit, splashing over Flynn's chest at the same time Boston groaned and molten lava filled Flynn's ass.

"Mmm," Malakai purred as he extracted his teeth from Flynn's shoulder. "Welcome home, sweetheart."

Unable to move, barely breathing, and not capable of coherent thought, Flynn just nodded weakly.

It was the best welcoming he'd ever received.

* * * *

"Does anyone in this house wear clothes?"

Boston chuckled under his breath as he eased out of Flynn's hole and looked over his shoulder to smile at Stavion. "I take it we're not the first you've walked in on?"

Stavion groaned and shook his head. "Xander was fucking Braxton in the hallway when I came out of your room. I swear I'm not lying when I say that they just waved at me and kept going."

Boston laughed again. "Yeah, that sounds about right." Returning his attention to his lovers, he helped a limp Malakai off of Flynn and cradled him in his lap. "Mmm, you smell like sex, baby."

"Stavion is staring at Flynn's dick." Malakai yawned and turned his face into Boston's chest as if he were commenting on nothing more important than the weather. "I can't be mad, though, it's such a nice dick."

"I'm not staring," Stavion mumbled, blushing to the tips of his ears. "Do you think you guys could put some clothes on? We need to talk."

Boston didn't like the sound of that. Nothing good ever came from those words. Grabbing one of the larger scraps that had been Flynn's T-shirt, he cleaned himself and his mates as best he could before slipping on his jeans and urging them to do the same.

"I still have cum dripping out of my ass," Malakai whined as he zipped his jeans. They'd finally gotten him a pair, and he looked damn good in them as far as Boston was concerned.

"We'll get you in the shower as soon as we hear what Stavion has to say." Boston kissed the vampire's temple then gave him a little shove toward the sofa. Turning to Flynn, he wrapped his arms around the man's corded neck and pressed their lips together. "How are you feeling, big guy?"

"Better. Ya take such good care of me." Flynn rubbed their cheeks together for a moment before kissing Boston once more and moving away. He settled down on the sofa, pulling Malakai into his lap and snaking his arm around Boston's waist when he sat down beside them. "Talk," he demanded of Stavion.

Boston tucked his long legs under him and curled into Flynn's side, running his hand over Malakai's hip while he listened to Stavion lay everything out for them. Apparently, a lot had been happening while they'd been waiting for Flynn to come home.

"The Enforcers were able to apprehend the werewolves along with the majority of the Montana coven. The coven leader, along with his personal guard, has disappeared. Since Blaise has taken over the Cloud Peak Pack and has two mates to take care of now, he has resigned his position as a Hunter."

Boston had never heard Stavion speak so formally. He was completely business, no trace or hint of a smile on his face. Hell, he barely even glanced at them as he spoke.

"This is hard for him," Malakai whispered inside his mind.

Boston gasped, completely forgetting that part of the mating bond. *"Can you hear me, too? Can Flynn hear us?"*

"Aye, I hear ya fine, my loves."

"Loves?" Malakai asked hesitantly through their bond. He squirmed around in Flynn's lap, staring intently into his eyes, before flickering his gaze to Boston and back again.

Boston knew he never wanted to be apart from Malakai, and thankfully now that they'd claimed each other, he wouldn't have to be. He still wasn't sure if what he felt was love or just a protectiveness for his new mate. Until he could work out his feelings, he didn't want to give Malakai false hope in case he discovered it was actually the latter.

"Is that why he's being so formal?" he asked instead, getting them back on the original topic before Flynn could say anything. He could feel the waves of love flowing off of Flynn for both him and Malakai. While it made his heart sing that Flynn could open himself up that way, he was afraid if Flynn bared his heart, they would expect Boston to follow suit.

"Yes. He lost two of his Enforcers. He's worried about me. He's ashamed that he didn't do more to keep Flynn safe. This is how he

deals with it—by shutting down. In his mind right now, he's here in an official capacity to deliver unpleasant news. Go easy on him."

There wasn't even a twinge of hurt in Malakai's tone as he slipped the words into Boston's mind. His eyes were soft and kind as he stared back, and Boston breathed a silent sigh of relief that he'd dodged the bullet for the time being.

"Are you even listening to me?" Stavion's fist came down on the coffee table, and he growled.

So much for Mr. Official Capacity. "I'm sorry, Stavion. You were saying?"

Stavion grumbled for another moment before he cleared his throat and shoved his hand through his hair.

"We have other Hunters and Trackers in the country, but none are as good as Blaise. It may take some time until we can catch up with these guys. It's unlikely that they'll come looking for you, but I want everyone to be on alert. Not all Trackers work for the I.C.P.J."

Until Logan's demon ex-girlfriend, and the subsequential need to call in Blaise, none of them had even heard of the International Council for Preternatural Justice. It had caused a lot of shit for them, including having to submit information about their pack for The Council Registry. Hell, Xander had even had to register Braxton and Keeton. Boston didn't like the elders having so much information about them, especially the fact that they were Moonlighters.

When all the craziness went down in Wyoming with Jackson's brother, Cole, and the following incident with Willow, it had only solidified his feelings that The Council had way too much information on the paranormals they were sworn to govern. Even after the elimination of the lunatic vampire, Cyrus Redway, Boston still didn't trust the other elders of The Council.

"He can't do that!" Malakai shouted.

"Not bloody happenin'!" Flynn roared.

Shit! Boston had obviously missed something important while he'd been off on his little internal tangent.

"I'm sorry," Stavion said, and he sounded like it. "Nicholas McCarthy is arguing that he offered the contract before you were mated, and that Elder Winters had no right to interfere. Technically, he's right." He groaned and wiped at his face while Boston's entire world came crashing down around him. "There's going to be a hearing."

"Where?" Boston croaked. He'd use every dirty trick in the book to keep Malakai with them.

"Wyoming. The elders are still there trying to help Blaise sort through the mess the previous alpha left."

"This is bullshit!" Flynn's chest heaved, and his arms tightened around both Malakai and Boston. "They'll not be takin' him."

Boston and Malakai looked at each other quickly before both reaching out to stroke and pet their irate lover. "Hush now," Malakai said softly. "They can't interfere with a mating bond. You know that. We're going to be fine, big guy."

Boston chanced a look at Stavion and didn't like what he saw. While he also assumed that a mating bond was the highest power in the land, apparently, he'd been wrong. Stavion looked sick to his stomach as he stared down at the carpet between his feet.

"We won't let anyone take him," Boston said with conviction as he pushed Flynn's dark hair back from his face and kissed his lips passionately. He gave Malakai the same treatment before dropping back to the cushions and panting heavily.

If he was willing to go to any extremes to keep Malakai with him—if his heart felt like it was shredding at the thought of losing him—did that mean that he loved the man?

Or could he blame his possessiveness on his mating instincts? Yeah, that sounded lame, even inside his own head. It was time to put up or shut up, and Boston had never been the strong and silent type.

Chapter Sixteen

"You need to feed before we leave."

Malakai cringed. Not because he didn't want to drink from his mate, but because he could feel the anxiety rolling off of Boston. While the man always put up a good front, now that they were mated, Malakai could feel every hint of hesitancy in the guy.

Boston always enjoyed his bite once it had taken place—Malakai made sure of it. But it was that initial grudging acceptance that he hated. The shifter was trying so hard, and Malakai knew Boston wanted him. Though, sometimes he had to wonder if Boston would have been as quick to claim him if someone else hadn't sought to take him.

He needed, and felt he deserved, someone who wanted him for all the right reasons. Wanting him just because someone else did wasn't a good enough reason in his eyes. "I'm fine. Let's just get this over with."

Boston frowned at him. Malakai could feel the hurt pouring from Boston now, and it only served to confuse the hell out of him. "I could get Flynn if you prefer."

Is he pouting? Malakai was never going to figure these big alphas out. "Boston, just tell me what you want." There, he'd said it. He was so damn tired and worried about the hearing that he just couldn't fake happy and mellow.

"Did I do something wrong?" The hurt grew stronger, and Malakai had to turn his back on his mate to hide the tears that stung at his eyes.

"Of course not," he managed to answer levelly.

"Then why won't you look at me?"

"Are ya ready then?" Flynn asked, stepping into the room. He took one look at Malakai's face and crossed the room to wrap him up in his big, powerful arms. "Ah, now, not to worry, little one." He placed kisses over the top of Malakai's head while he rubbed his back. "We'll not be letting that bloody idiot take ya away from us."

All Malakai could feel from Flynn was warmth, acceptance, and a fierce protectiveness to keep him safe at all costs. Flynn never held any part of himself back or made Malakai feel like he was unwanted because of what he was. He wished he could say the same for Boston. While he knew the man cared for him, there was still a part of Boston that hadn't fully accepted Malakai as his mate. Malakai wasn't sure if he ever would, and the knowledge felt like a sledgehammer to his chest.

"Do ya need a nip, my darlin'?"

Whatever his issues with Boston, Malakai wouldn't hurt his mate that way. After refusing to take blood from Boston, it would be a slap in the face if he accepted Flynn's offer. "No, but thank you. I'm fine, but a little worried about what's going to happen."

A warm, hard body pressed against his back, and Boston's lips trailed over his nape. "Nothing is going to happen, Malakai. You're too important, and we're not letting you go."

Malakai melted. It was the first thing Boston had said to him that showed that he might want Malakai for a reason besides the fact that they were mated. It wasn't a declaration of love, but it was a step in the right direction. It wasn't like Malakai was laying his heart out on the table, either.

"Let's get this over with." Malakai didn't think there was anything McCarthy could do to make the elders overturn their decision, but that didn't stop him from being nervous.

Flynn squeezed him and stepped away to open the door to their hotel room, but Boston didn't release his hold. He clutched Malakai to him, his body practically vibrating as he buried his face in the back of

Malakai's neck. "I'm not letting you go. Nothing they can say is going to change that."

Though Boston's words had Malakai falling just a little further in love with the man, the panic and desperation in his voice broke his heart. Looking up at Flynn, he pleaded with his eyes as he pushed his thoughts at his mate. *"What do I do? How do I help him?"*

Flynn smiled that special smile that always turned Malakai to putty. *"Just be honest and speak the truth. Tell him what's in ya heart."*

Malakai shook his head fractionally. He wasn't ready for that. While he hated knowing his mate was in pain, he couldn't put himself out there and declare his undying love when Boston couldn't even fully accept him.

Instead, he turned in Boston's arms and pressed their mouths together, throwing all of his feelings into the kiss that he couldn't verbalize. As their tongues twined together and Boston crushed him against his muscled chest, Malakai knew it wouldn't be long before all his walls came crumbling down, and he'd take Boston anyway he could get him.

* * * *

"Leader McCarthy claims that the contract was offered in writing before the mating of Malakai Bruins to Boston Mackey and Flynn Murphy. Is this true, Leader Shogard?" Elder Macintosh, the shifter representative of The Council addressed Stavion from the small dais where he and the other elders—except Elder Winters—perched.

Malakai sat between his mates, holding each of their hands in a white-knuckled grip. Sweat beaded across his forehead and his stomach rolled uncomfortably. Glancing to his left, he met Elder Winters' eyes and tried to return the man's smile. He didn't think he quite made it, though, when Boston leaned over and kissed his damp forehead.

"Relax, baby."

Yeah, that was easy for Boston to say. If The Council ruled in favor of Nicholas McCarthy, not only would Malakai be forced to leave his mates, but Stavion would be in deep shit as well. He didn't even know this fucking creep. Why couldn't the guy just leave him alone?

"Yes," Stavion answered clearly. He held his head high with his shoulders back, and Malakai envied his friend's confidence, even if it was just for show.

"Yet, you petitioned Elder Winters to allow the trio more time to claim one another."

"Actually, I petitioned the elder," Blaise spoke up, rising from his seat and going to stand beside Stavion. "Flynn Murphy is an Enforcer, sir, and was away on an assignment. They had only met when he was called away."

"I understand this, Alpha Taylor, but that does not excuse the fact that Leader Shogard purposely withheld the acceptance of the contract knowing that Mr. Bruins was unmated."

"On the contrary," Blaise said genially. "Though Malakai may have been unclaimed, he was very much mated. I'm sure as a shifter, you understand."

Elder Macintosh huffed and grumbled under his breath. Malakai didn't take that as a good sign. He knew Blaise was only trying to help, but he wished the man would sit down and shut his damn mouth. All he was doing was pissing off the elder. No authority figure liked having their underlings telling them how to do their jobs.

McCarthy turned in his seat and winked at Malakai. Boston must have seen it, because he shifted forward in his seat and snarled.

"Easy, *moi chroí*," Flynn whispered, looping his fingers around the back of Boston's neck and squeezing.

Keeping a tight hold on Flynn's hand, Malakai moved closer to Boston's side, hoping to calm the man further. Thankfully, it worked, because Boston settled back in his seat and kissed Malakai's temple.

He didn't take his menacing glare off the back of McCarthy's head, though.

"Elder, I can provide proof that I offered the mating contract a full month before Leader Shogard ever responded. It is my understanding that Mr. Bruins did not arrive in Georgia to meet his mates until several weeks afterward."

Malakai's attention went from McCarthy to Stavion. If what the man said was true, they were so completely fucked. All that time, and Stavion never mentioned a word. Why would his friend keep something like that from him?"

"Is this true?" Elder Means, the lycan representative asked.

"Yes," Stavion offered tightly after a brief hesitation. "However, while it is true that Malakai did not meet Mr. Murphy until his arrival in Georgia, he did have a brief meeting with Mr. Mackey several months prior."

Malakai knew it was the wrong thing to say the minute Stavion started speaking. His head started to pound, and he suddenly couldn't get enough air into his lungs.

"So, there was ample time for him to be claimed by his *mates*," McCarthy argued, his voice laced with honey. "If Mr. Mackey did not want his mate, I do not see the problem with the mating contract."

Malakai didn't like the way McCarthy said "mates." There was something off about it, as though it left a bitter taste on his tongue.

Elder Macintosh took his glasses off and rubbed at his eyes for a minute before he replaced them and sighed. "He's right, Stavion," the elder spoke, dropping all formalities. "I'm sorry, but I have no choice but to rule in favor of Nicholas McCarthy and grant approval for his contract."

"But they're bonded!" Blaise shouted. "You can't do that!"

"I'm sorry," Elder Macintosh repeated. "Without a vampire representative for The Council, my hands are tied."

Malakai's five-five frame shook violently as McCarthy's personal guards swaggered toward him with evil smirks on their faces.

"No!" Flynn and Boston roared in unison, jumping to their feet and launching themselves at the guards.

Malakai couldn't move as he watched not only Boston and Flynn, but Blaise and Stavion fight against the guards. He knew they couldn't win, though. Twelve Council Guards rushed in through the side doors, quickly dominating the situation and subduing Malakai's friends and mates.

He finally found his legs when one of McCarthy's guards advanced on him. Shooting to his feet, he tried to run, but the man was bigger and faster, catching Malakai around the waist and hauling him off his feet.

"No!" Malakai kicked and flailed, screaming at the top of his lungs as the guard carried him back to where McCarthy waited.

Boston and Flynn were still growling and snarling as they struggled against the guards in their attempts to get to Malakai. "Let me go!" Malakai reached for his mates as he passed them, his heart shattering inside his chest. "I love you," he choked out. "I love you both so much. I'm sorry."

Then something sharp pricked his arm and everything went black.

* * * *

"Malakai!" Boston fought vehemently against the two guards holding him as he watched his mate's limp body being passed off to McCarthy.

This couldn't be happening. It wasn't right. Malakai was theirs!

Flynn struggled against his own set of guards as he shouted Malakai's name. Malakai's fear, Flynn's fury, and Boston's own agonizing emotions swirled inside him, making it impossible for him to clear his head enough to shift. And what the fuck was he going to do if he did? He was a goddamn deer. He didn't have fangs or claws. Granted, he did have antlers, but he also imagined the guards would have him shot and mounted on the wall before he even finished his shift.

McCarthy gave them a wide grin before dipping his head and pressing his lips to Malakai's forehead. Cold, unadulterated rage settled over Boston, but before he could shift, one of the guards stepped forward and jabbed a needle into the side of his neck.

"Motherfucker!" he roared. It wasn't a tranquilizer, but an Inhibitor, a drug specially designed by The Council to prevent the transformation in shifters. Another guard stuck Flynn, and even Blaise was catching a needle to the neck. Apparently, these guys weren't taking any chances.

It was smart of them, because if Boston got free, he was going to tear them all apart slowly.

"Flynn, what the fuck do we do?"

"I don't know, a ghrá, but we'll get him back. I'm feelin' the same about him as ya do."

"I love you, Flynn. You and Malakai are everything to me. I can't let that monster have him."

"Don't be startin' with the goodbyes, darlin'. I love ya, too, but ya need to be usin' that head God gave ya."

Boston was trying, but he couldn't think around the devastation to his heart. They were going to lose Malakai all because he'd been a stupid son of a bitch.

McCarthy looked up at him again, staring right into his eyes, and gave him a satisfied smirk as if he'd won some rare and grand prize—which he had. Malakai was a precious treasure, and he belonged to Boston.

McCarthy winked at him, and Boston went crazy, screaming and redoubling his efforts to free himself from the men holding him. Flynn and Stavion were putting up a good fight as well, but they were outnumbered and overpowered.

As he watched his mate disappear, Boston stilled his struggles,and the heavy weight of despair settled over him. He'd lost. He'd failed both of his mates by not being able to pull his head out of his ass and see what was right in front of him until it was too late.

The doors at the back of the room banged open and his entire pack spilled into the room, including Keeton and Braxton. Even Blaise's mates, Cole and Willow, were with them, and they all had huge smiles on their faces.

"Wait!" Xander shouted, and everyone went still. Though the alpha was normally as laid-back as they come, when he was angry, he exuded so much power, everyone fell over themselves to do as he said. He jerked his head toward McCarthy, and Jackson, Talon, and Logan all stepped forward, making their way toward the vampire.

McCarthy's guards surrounded him, crouching low as they bared their fangs and prepared to defend their leader. Then the side door opened and five very large men that looked a hell of a lot like Flynn stepped into the room, subduing the guards before anyone could blink.

Boston looked to Blaise, and the man grinned broadly at him. "I was hoping they'd make it in time. I figured you could use a little Murphy magic. It wasn't easy finding Flynn's brothers."

Boston jerked his head toward Flynn, but before he could demand an explanation, Stavion's Enforcers came through the other set of doors behind the dais and marched across the room to take up ranks beside Xander. Boston didn't know what the fuck was going on, but he'd never been so glad to see so many people on his side.

"What is the meaning of this?" Elder Macintosh shouted. "This is a private hearing, and my judgment is final!"

"Oh, blow it out your ass, Samuel." Elder Winters rose to his feet and went to stand on Xander's other side. "This is bullshit, and you know it."

Talon took the moment while everyone was distracted to plow his fist into McCarthy's face and snatch Malakai out of his arms. Then he walked across the room, smiling the entire way, and gently placed

Malakai into Boston's arms. "You really need to learn how to ask for help, brother."

Clutching his mate to him, he dipped his head in gratitude, unable to speak through the constriction of his throat. He was racking up IOUs all over the place, but it didn't matter. He'd spend every day of his life doing whatever he had to do to pay his family back. And it was more than just his pack. Malakai was his family, and by extension, Stavion and the other Enforcers.

"Flynn, ya be owin' us for this," one of the newcomers yelled before elbowing one of McCarthy's guards in the ribs. "How is it ya always be getting' into the most trouble?"

"I've been missin' ya, too, Devlin, and a sight for sore eyes ya are."

"And what are ya havin' to say to the rest of us?" another of them asked, kicking his foot out nonchalantly to connect with one of the guards on the ground. He looked down at the guy and smirked. "I'm thinkin' I'll be likin' America just fine."

"So, are ya stayin' then?" A big goofy smile spread over Flynn's face as he shook the guards' hold off and moved over to wrap his arms around Boston and Malakai. He kissed Boston first, then pressed his lips to Malakai's forehead. "What would ya say to havin' a big family, darlin'?"

"You know these guys?" Well, that had been a stupid question. Blaise had just said they were Flynn's brothers. Wow, he really needed to think before he opened his mouth.

Flynn kept smiling and dipped his head. "Have I never told ya about my brothers?"

"No, but I'm just glad you have so many." Boston gave the men a smile and a nod of his head before he turned back to Flynn and claimed his lips in a scorching kiss. "I love you, Flynn."

"Aye, I know ya do." Flynn chuckled when Boston rolled his eyes. "And ya know I love you, too."

"Better."

"Excuse me!" Elder Macintosh shouted, his face mottling red with anger. "Who are these people? What are they doing here?"

McCarthy opened his mouth to offer his own protest, but Devlin gave him a frightening glare, and the man snapped his lips closed. Boston liked his mate's brothers already.

"Nicholas McCarthy has no claim to Malakai," Cole said, pushing through the crowd to stand in front of Xander. Raven and Varik moved in behind him, and the big vampirescrossed their arms over their chest, daring anyone to mess with the little shifter.

"The contract is binding," Elder Means said quietly. "I wish it weren't so, but our hands are tied."

Boston wanted to punch the smug look right off of McCarthy's face. Before Boston could get too worked up, Devlin's hand came out and connected solidly with the back of the coven leader's head. Then he crossed his arms over his chest again as if nothing had happened. Yeah, Boston could definitely tell they were related to Flynn.

"The mating contract must be presented to the coven leader, right?"

"Yes," Elder Macintosh said slowly, but his voice had lost some of its heat. Now, he just sounded confused, and maybe a little irritated.

"Stavion Shogard is not Malakai's coven leader," Willow said hurriedly from Blaise's arms. "None of the Enforcers swore an oath to Stavion."

"Nor have they been released from the leader of the Snake River Coven," Cole added with a self-satisfied smirk.

"Is this true?" Elder Means asked, looking toward Raven and Varik since Malakai was still passed out.

"Yes, sir," Raven said clearly. "We will follow Stavion anywhere, and we fully intend to become members of his coven, but we have not sworn our oaths yet."

Everyone was quiet for several minutes before Elder Macintosh rubbed his hands over his face and stood. "If no one has anything further to add, then I hereby declare the contract null and void. Malakai is to stay with his mates." The elder looked over at Flynn and Boston and smiled crookedly. "Congratulations, gentlemen."

"I have a question," one of Flynn's brothers announced. Boston didn't know their names, but he figured they'd make their introductions later. "Why the bloody hell does he want my brother's mate?"

All eyes turned toward McCarthy. "He is very beautiful," the vampire answered with a strange look on his face. "I was captivated from the moment I laid eyes on him."

"That's no reason to try and buy *my* mate!" Boston yelled at him. "You're fucking crazy. Stay away from us, or I will kill you and laugh while I do it."

"He doesn't belong to you!" McCarthy exploded. "He's mine!" He made a move toward them, but one of his own guards wrapped his hands around the leader and held him back.

"He is not yours!"

"He is mine. You took him from me." McCarthy struggled against the man holding him. "I love him!"

If Boston hadn't been holding Malakai in his arms, he would have been across the room and driving his fist into the asshole's face. "You met him once. How crazy are you?"

"He's mine! The mating contract was the only way to get him back after you took him from me!"

"Enough!" the guard holding McCarthy shouted. He transferred his leader to one of the other guards and mumbled something to him. Then he walked forward as though facing a firing squad and stood before the elders with his shoulders slumped. "This is my fault."

"How do you mean, Jonas?" Elder Means asked.

Boston leaned closer to Flynn so he could speak quietly and still be heard. "Who is that? What's going on?"

Flynn shook his head slowly, but his eyes were narrowed on the guard's back.

"Nicholas McCarthy is my mate," Jonas said dejectedly. "He refused to accept the bond, however."

"That's a lie!" McCarthy shouted. Everyone ignored him.

"I don't understand," Elder Macintosh said and pinched the bridge of his nose. "What does that have to do with this hearing?"

"While my main Enforcer duties are to protect Leader McCarthy, I do occasionally accept assignments from The Council."

Elder Winters nodded as he strolled forward to stand beside Jonas, the picture of ease. "You were given an assignment just a few months ago. I understand that it was not successful."

Boston was becoming more confused by the minute. He just wanted to take his mates and get the hell out of the place. How was any of this his problem?

Jonas took a deep breath and let it out slowly before addressing the remaining elders seated on the dais. "The assignment was to bring a witch into custody and present her before The Council for misuse of her powers." He paused and glanced over at McCarthy. "I let her go."

Gasps went around the room, and Boston rolled his eyes. "I wish he'd just get on with it," he grumbled out of the side of his mouth to Flynn.

"You released her?" Elder Macintosh sounded appalled. "Why would you do that?"

"I made a deal with her. If she could cast a spell to make Nicholas love me, I would release her and inform The Council that she'd bewitched me and escaped."

"Oh, Jonas." Elder Winters shook his head sadly. "She tricked you, didn't she?"

"Yes," Jonas growled. "She cast the spell so that Nicholas would fall in love with the first person he set eyes on. That was the day that he met Malakai Bruins. The first man to walk into his office after the spell was cast."

No one spoke for a long time, and Boston finally began to understand the magnitude of what the vampire had done. This wasn't just going to cost him his job. There would be major consequences.

The elders bent their heads together and spoke amongst themselves for several minutes before returning their attention to Jonas.

"Why did you not bring this information forward before now?" Elder Means asked.

Jonas chuckled darkly. "I like my head right where it is, thank you very much. It was selfish, but I have no desire to go to jail." He scrubbed as his face and sighed. "This has gone too far, though. I take full responsibility."

Elder Winters looked sad as he spoke. "Your trial will be set, and you can plead your case then."

Jonas shook his head. "I'd rather just get this over with."

Flynn patted Boston's arm and crossed the room to stand beside Jonas. "I'm thinkin' I might have a suggestion that'll be to everyone's likin'."

The corners of Elder Winters' lips twitched, and he nodded for Flynn to continue. Boston liked the elder. He wasn't a self-centered, power-hungry jerk like the others. What the hell was Flynn up to, though?

"Well, ya be needin' to find a witch to break this spell. McCarthy will be needin' someone to watch over 'im in the meantime, 'cause I won't be havin' him comin' for Malakai." The slight growl in his voice made Boston shiver and his dick twitch in interest.

"What are you suggesting?" Elder Means asked as he leaned back in his chair and crossed his arms over his chest. "Leader McCarthy hasn't technically done anything wrong to warrant punishment."

"Aye, but he's been cursed, and he'll need watchin'." Flynn glanced over his shoulder and winked at Boston. "Ya have a fine Enforcer here, and I'm thinkin' you'll not want to be wastin' his talents."

"I haven't been cursed," McCarthy grumbled. "I love Malakai. He belongs to me, and this is just some elaborate scheme to take him away."

Flynn's brother, Devlin, reached out and smacked McCarthy in the back of the head again. "Mind ya tongue."

Boston had a feeling he was really going to like these guys. He smirked a little, but quickly snapped his attention back to the front when Elder Winters began to speak again.

"So, we place Leader McCarthy in Jonas's care until we can find a way to break the curse." Elder Winters smiled and bobbed his head. "Any infractions committed during that time will of course be sanctioned against Jonas. He will also be in charge of locating the witch and reversing the charm."

Boston didn't know how he felt about the idea. He'd worry about it later. He just wished they'd wrap it up already.

"Well, since you want to do my job for me, I guess I'm not needed here," Elder Macintosh said in a huff to Flynn.

"Ah, but you'd be realizin' it on ya own, Elder." Flynn gave the man a winsome smile. "I was just wantin' to ease ya burden. Ya be a fine elder."

Suspicion flittered over Elder Macintosh's face before his lips split into a wide grin. "Fine. Unless my fellow Council members have any complaints, I hereby name Enforcer Jonas Tracer guardian of Leader Nicholas McCarthy until such time as he can find a way to reverse this confounded spell."

He looked around the room, his gaze lingering on McCarthy for a moment as though he expected the man to argue further. When no one spoke, he dipped his head and rose from his seat. "Dismissed."

Jackson shuffled over and bumped Boston's shoulder with his own. "He's good," he said with a nod toward Flynn's back.

Boston snorted and rolled his eyes. "That's Irish diplomacy for you."

"Huh?"

"The ability to tell someone to go to hell and make them happy to be going."

Jackson thought it over for a minute before bursting into laughter. "Are you ready to go home?"

"Definitely. Get me the hell out of here." If Boston ever stepped foot in Wyoming again, it would be too soon. He had a lot to make up for, a lot of groveling to do, and hopefully a lot of makeup sex on his schedule.

He couldn't wait to get started.

Chapter Seventeen

"I hope you don't mind that I called your brothers." Blaise settled onto the sofa in the common room of their hotel suite as he addressed Flynn. "They were already here, and I figured you could use all the backup you could get."

Looking around the room, seeing his brothers, his friends, his mates' families gathered around them, Flynn felt like the luckiest bastard on earth. "I'm grateful to ya, Blaise. I'm indebted to ya and your mates."

As much as he wanted to kick everyone out and love on his mates, he also wanted to kick everyone out and spend time with his brothers. "I've missed ya, brothers."

"Aye, and we've missed ya as well." Devlin gave him a brief one-arm hug before stepping aside so that Flynn's other brothers could greet him as well.

"Uh, well, we're just going to go, umm..." Talon trailed off, looking uncertain.

"I'm starving," Jackson piped up with a quick wink to Flynn. "You haven't even fed me today."

Talon rolled his eyes and snorted. "C'mon, pup. It's been a whole three hours since you've eaten. I'm sure you're about to fade away."

"Aww, you get me." Jackson pecked his mate on the lips and led the way out of the room with a little wave.

Everyone laughed as they followed the kid's lead and dipped out of the room to give Flynn some privacy with his brothers.

"Malakai's still out in the bedroom." Boston jerked a thumb over his shoulder to indicate the slightly open door behind him. "I'll go grab us some burgers and be back in a little while."

He stretched up for a brief kiss, but Flynn wrapped his lover up in his arms and kissed him to within an inch of his life. "Stay."

"Okay," Boston answered dazedly as he stared at Flynn's mouth. His hard cock pressed against Flynn's hip, and his soft, pink tongue darted out to wet his lips.

Flynn's brothers snickered to themselves, holding their hands up in surrender when Flynn shot them a scathing look. Christ, his sweet mate looked good enough to eat. Maybe he could postpone his talk with his family.

"Ya did good, Flynn. Ya have two fine mates."

"So, have ya found your mates then?"

While most answered no, the twins, Cian and Farren held hands and answered in the affirmative. Flynn gaped at them in horror until the runts fell together, laughing their fool heads off. "We're just messin' with ya, Flynn," Cian gasped through his amusement. "Ah, ya should see your face."

"Knock it off ya two. We've not seen Flynn in years, and this how ya choose to be greetin' 'im?" Devlin sighed and shook his head at the two troublemakers before looking at Flynn once more. "I'm sorry for the troubles ya had, Flynn. I'd have been there for ya if I'd known."

"Wait," Boston said, holding his hand up. "You didn't know that Flynn had been kidnapped?"

Flynn could feel the anger rolling off his mate, but it wasn't his brothers' fault. He'd run away from home, refusing to follow in his Da's and Devlin's footsteps. Ironic that he'd left home because he hadn't wanted to become an Enforcer, and that's exactly what he'd ended up doing anyway.

He hadn't told anyone he was leaving, nor where he was going. It had been nearly a year after he'd left Ireland before he was kidnapped, and he hadn't spoken to any of his family during that time. After he'd been freed from his captivity, he'd been too ashamed to turn to his family for help.

Pulling Boston to him, he stroked his lover's back as he explained everything to him. Boston calmed, relaxing into Flynn's embrace as he nuzzled his nose against Flynn's neck. "I'm sorry, love. I hate what happened to you, and I hate that you did it to protect me."

This started a whole new round of questions, and Flynn held Boston tight as he relived his painful memories from the time spent in that basement. "They wanted Boston," he said in a flat monotone. "I wasn't goin' to let that happen." Then he skimmed over the rape and abuse, not going into great detail about it. They were his scars, but he'd learned to move past them. Knowing that he'd done it to protect that man he loved went a long way in healing him.

"Ma is gonna have ya hide," Oisin snickered. Leave it to the youngest of them to find the humor in any situation.

"I'm sorry, who are you?" Boston asked curiously.

"Ah, sorry there, Boston." Flynn felt like a shit for not introducing everyone earlier. "These are my brothers, Devlin, Oisin, Cian, Farren, and Bannon." He pointed out each man as he said their names. "And this is my *a ghrá*, Boston Mackey."

"Wow, look at all those muscles," came a sleepy voice from behind them.

Flynn turned, beaming a mile wide as Malakai shuffled over to them. Instead of moving apart, Flynn pulled Malakai down so that he sat on one of his thighs and one of Boston's. "This beauty is our mate, Malakai Bruins."

"Aye, and a finer man I've never seen," Cian answered, raking his eyes over Malakai's naked chest.

"If ya want to keep them eyes, ya'll be puttin' 'em back in ya head, Cian Murphy." Flynn wrapped a possessive arm around Malakai and snarled.

Malakai turned his head and kissed Flynn's jaw. "Oh, I do love it when you get all growly." He turned the other way and pecked Boston on the lips. "There's my sunshine," he purred.

"Uh, baby, are you feeling okay?" Boston glanced up at Flynn, yelping when Malakai reached down cup his groin.

"I don't know," Malakai answered distractedly, moving his other hand down to massage Flynn's cock through his jeans. "I feel kind of funny, and really, really hot. My dick is all swollen, too." Stretching his neck up, he caught Flynn's bottom lip between his teeth and tugged. "I think it needs a kiss."

Devlin cleared his throat, but Malakai just looked over at him and winked. "You can watch if you want."

Flynn almost swallowed his tongue. He'd never seen Malakai like this, and while he didn't want his brothers watching him have sex, his dick definitely liked this side of his little mate.

Shaking his head and smirking as he stood and gathered his brothers, Devlin looked over at Flynn and winked. "We'll have us a talk later. Enjoy ya mates for now."

"Wait." Flynn tried to think around the pounding of his heart and the throbbing in his dick. "How long a ya stayin'?"

"We're bein' transferred," Bannon answered excitedly. "We're all volunteerin' for it, of course, but we'll be talkin' later." His eyes went to Malakai's hand as it slipped inside Boston's jeans. "Right, I think we'll be leavin' now."

The minute his brothers were out of the room, Flynn was on his feet and stripping out of his clothes. "Naked," he growled.

Boston's movements were frantic as he worked to divest his clothing as well. Malakai giggled, wiggling his hips as he shimmied out of his sleep pants and lounged back on the sofa with his legs spread wide. He held his arms open to them and wiggled his fingers.

Flynn and Boston shared a quick look before diving to the floor and attacking every inch of skin they could reach on Malakai's body with their lips, tongues, and hands. "I so deserve this after the day I had." Malakai moaned, arching his back and pushing his hips closer to their searching mouths.

Capturing the engorged head of his mate's cock, Flynn closed his eyes and groaned as Malakai's sweet taste burst over his taste buds. Boston disappeared, but was back moments later with a travel-sized bottle of lube grasped in his hand.

Popping the cap open, he liberally coated his fingers, lifted Malakai's leg higher, and slicked his perfect little hole. No one spoke, but their moans and growls filled the room and echoed off the walls.

Flynn sucked harder, dragging his lips along Malakai's pulsing length as he watch Boston insert two fingers into their mate's fluttering hole. The digits sawed in and out, and Flynn picked up his pace, matching the rhythm Boston set.

"I think our dirty little mate needs to be reminded who's in charge." Boston added a third finger and twisted his wrist. "Maybe he needs to be punished."

"Yes, please. I was so bad," Malakai panted. "Spank me, fuck me, whatever you want, just don't stop."

If his men kept it up with their naughty words, Flynn was going to blow his load all over the floor instead of inside a hot, wet orifice. Extracting his fingers, Boston gave Flynn just enough time to pull off Malakai's cock before he pulled the man down into his lap. Resting his back against the front of the sofa, he lowered Malakai over his cock, and pulled their lover back so that his back pressed against Boston's chest.

Flynn grabbed the base of his cock to keep from shooting as he watched Malakai's tight ass eat up Boston's cock. They were so fucking beautiful, and they were all his.

"Flynn, get over here and let our baby suck your cock," Boston demanded, planting his feet on the floor and thrusting up into Malakai's willing tunnel.

Not willing to miss the opportunity, Flynn scrambled to his feet and straddled Boston's thighs, spreading his legs until his weeping crown lined up with Malakai's mouth. Rubbing the tip over his lover's lips, he growled in appreciation when they glistened with his pre-cum. "Open up, *mo chroí*."

Bless his heart, Malakai gave him a sexy little grin and opened right up, engulfing half of Flynn's hard cock into his moist mouth. Dropping his head back, he let go of all his stress and just enjoyed the feel of his lover's tongue stroking over his aching dick.

Resting a hand on the top of Malakai's head, he thrust gently, working his slippery length through the man's plump lips. Just when he was getting into it, Boston demanded they stop. Flynn wanted to growl in frustration, until Boston lifted Malakai off his cock and settled him on his knees with his chest pressed again the couch cushions.

"Fuck his ass, but no coming."

Flynn didn't want to examine too closely why Boston's commanding voice had his dick flexing and his ass clenching greedily. Dropping to his knees, he grabbed the lube and slicked his cock before spreading Malakai's ass cheeks and pushing inside of him until he was buried balls deep in his mate's tight ass.

"Ah, sweet hell, darlin'." Curling his fingers around Malakai's hips, Flynn slammed into him, thrusting hard and fast as he chased his orgasm. The needy moans and whimpers falling from Malakai's mouth made him feel like a god.

Reaching around to stroke Malakai's bouncing prick, Flynn froze when Boston growled. "No coming!"

Jerking his head around to peer at his lover, Flynn's thrusts faltered and his hold on Malakai's hips turned bruising. Boston was sprawled on the floor, jerking his gorgeous cock and pumping three fingers into his pretty pucker. "Ya tryin' to kill me," Flynn sobbed.

"Ready," Boston announced, flipping over to his hands and knees and crawling toward them. "I'm going to fuck Malakai's sweet little hole while you bury that beautiful dick in my ass."

"Oh, yes!" Malakai cried. "Hurry. Do it!

Flynn could only nod numbly as he pulled out of Malakai and watched Boston slide into position. Watching over the man's shoulder, he had to squeeze his cock again at the glorious sight.

"Flynn, are you going to fuck me, or are you just going to watch?"

"Either way, I need to come," Malakai added. His cheeky remark earned him a swat on his ass from Boston. Malakai moaned like a high-dollar whore and wiggled his hips. "More. Please, do that again."

Flynn couldn't move as he watched Boston pound into Malakai's ass as he spanked him. Seeing his little vampire's pale skin burn a scorching red from Boston's hand had him so cranked up, he could barely breathe. Who knew he'd be into such things? Maybe he'd look into getting them some toys when they got home.

"Close," Boston grunted, snapping Flynn out of temporary paralysis.

"Not without me, ya not." Molding himself to Boston's back, he lined up and pushed home roughly, roaring at the feel of Boston's muscles stretched tight around his throbbing dick. He snapped, all sense of self-control vanished, and he plowed into Boston's ass at a furious pace.

Making use of his long arms, he draped them around Boston and gripped Malakai's hips as he continued his assault of Boston's ass. Then his mates started moving with him, catching up to his demanding tempo, and Flynn's vision dimmed as his orgasm rocketed through him.

Boston roared, Malakai screamed, and Flynn dropped his forehead to Boston's damp shoulder and groaned as he unloaded his balls, filling his mate's depths with his hot seed. Boston's inner walls clamped around him, squeezing him, and Flynn wanted to sob with joy and relief.

He had his men. They were together, unharmed, and happy. "I love you," he whispered into Boston's ear.

"What about me?" Malakai asked inside his head. Flynn wasn't sure if he was meant to hear it or not, but he wouldn't pass up the opportunity to tell his little mate exactly how he felt. He might not have known Malakai long, but the man had wiggled right into his heart with his bubbly personality and giving soul.

He waited until they'd all pulled apart before pulling Malakai into his lap and kissing him passionately. "I love you, *mo chroí.*"

"What does that mean?"

"My heart," Boston whispered, sitting down beside them on the carpet and ghosting his lips up the side of the Malakai's neck. "I love you, too, sweetheart. Did you mean it when you said it back at the hearing?"

The fear and uncertainty drifting off of Boston made Flynn's heart ache. He had a feeling it wouldn't last long, though.

Craning his neck, Malakai captured Boston's lips in a sweet, tender kiss. "Yes. I love you, Boston." He turned and looked up at Flynn. "And you, big guy. Is that okay? I mean, I know we haven't been together very long, but I can't imagine I will ever feel this way about anyone. I love you both, so much."

"More than okay." Sure enough, the feelings Flynn was getting from Boston were now warm and fuzzy. It was almost nauseating how happy he was. It probably would have been if Flynn wasn't feeling the exact same way.

"Ya heart knows what it wants," Flynn tried to explain. "How long were ya knowin' Stavion before he became your best friend?"

Malakai's brows drew together, and he tilted his head to the side. "Almost instantly. He was always there for me. I don't love him like you guys, but I do love him. I'd do anything I could to help him."

Boston smiled and nodded. "Did you question your friendship with him? Or that you loved him like a brother, though you hadn't known each other very long?"

His eyes lit up, and Malakai shook his head slowly. "I see what you're saying."

"When it's right, it just fits, and you *know* it," Boston added. "Don't be scared of it. I think it's wonderful. I'm happier than I can ever remember being."

Some of the brightness dimmed in Malakai's eyes, and he scooted around in Flynn's lap to face Boston. "Are you sure that's how you really feel? Or is it because you almost lost me? I know you still get scared when I bite you. I love you, Boston, but I need someone to love all of me—not just pieces of me. These"—He tapped at one of his canines—"are parts of me, too, whether you like it or not."

Boston never stopped smiling as he held out his arms and waited for Malakai to go to him. Flynn thought he was going to burst with pride and happiness. This is all he'd ever wanted. One mate would have been enough for him, but having Malakai in their life was like a breath of fresh air he never knew he'd been missing.

"I'm not scared anymore, Malakai. I was fighting so hard because I was scared. Not of your pointy little teeth, but scared of loving you. You have no idea what it does to me to know that I can provide something for you. Your bite is the hottest thing in the world." He glanced up at Flynn and smiled sheepishly. "Sorry, big guy."

Flynn waved him away with a mirroring smile. He knew exactly what Boston meant. While he loved the feeling of Boston's teeth on him, knowing they belonged together, Malakai's bite was mind-melting. Maybe it was a vampire thing. Whatever it was, Flynn couldn't get enough of it, and apparently, neither could Boston.

"When Flynn came back into my life, I was still struggling to let him in. My world has been one endless midnight for so long. Then Flynn shows up, and it's like this tiny ray of sunlight trying to peek through the darkness."

"Boston, my world is always going to be midnight," Malakai said quietly. "I won't ever be able to meet you for lunch, or go to the beach and lounge in the sun. It's still one endless night with me."

"I've always preferred the night," Boston said with a wink, and Flynn could feel the truth in his words.

"Same here," he added. There was something so peaceful about running through the night with the moon and stars shining down on him.

"You're not just saying that?" Malakai's head whipped back and forth to look at them both several times.

"No," they both answered in stereo.

"Malakai you blew into my world like a cyclone and shook everything up. You opened up my heart, and all the sudden I was filled with light. You saved me." Boston kissed Malakai's lips sweetly. "You broke down all my walls so I could not only let you in, but Flynn as well. I don't know what I'd ever do without either of you."

"You'll never have to find out," Malakai answered and sniffled.

"Ya two are it for me, *a ghrá*. I'm not needin' the day when I have my own personal sunshine here in my arms."

Malakai's eyes shimmered with tears, but the love pouring from his soul was enough to bring grown men to their knees. Good thing Flynn was already sitting down. "Show me," Malakai purred seductively.

"Ah, with pleasure, my love."

Epilogue

They never left Wyoming. The one place in the world Boston never wanted to step foot again, and now he lived there. He'd called and had his and Flynn's things shipped to Stavion's estate—their home for the past three months.

The pack house was great, and he'd miss his family, but it wasn't conducive for having a vampire mate—or having two mates for that matter. There just wasn't enough room, and Malakai needed the safety that living with his coven provided.

In the end, it had been an easy decision to make. Boston would always put his men's needs before his own. He had a new family now, Malakai and the Enforcers had finally pledged their allegiance to Stavion, and they'd renamed the coven as the Haven Coven.

"Raven and Demos are bringing in more tonight," Malakai said as if reading his thoughts. "This place really is like a sanctuary for all the misfits out there."

It wasn't just vampires. Shifters, elves, even misplaced werewolves were invited to live with the coven as long as they abided by their laws. So far, no one had made waves. The Council was still working with Blaise and Cole to find and rescue all the paranormals Cole's dad had sold or traded. The work was taxing on both the mind and body, but they all felt it was worth it.

Flynn was able to keep his job as an Enforcer, but now guarded the compound along with his brothers. Boston was just happy that his lover was never sent out into the field.

"They found 'em!" Flynn shouted, bursting through the door and lifting Boston off his feet to swing him around. "The coven leader and his guards, my brothers found 'em!"

"That's fantastic!" Malakai yelled, jumping up from the sofa and rushing to throw his arms around them both. "Oh, I'm so happy for you two. You can finally have a little peace."

Boston couldn't breathe. The relief that slammed into him at the information would have dropped him like a ton of bricks if Flynn wasn't holding him up. "Bannon found him?"

"Aye, Stavion says Bannon is a damn fine Tracker, the best he's ever met."

"Is that why Blaise asked them to come here?" Boston was grateful that Flynn had his brothers, but he still wondered why they'd chosen to leave their homeland to come to America.

"Jackson found out about Flynn's brothers when he was working with The Council database," Malakai explained quietly. "He told Blaise, Blaise told Stavion, and Stavion called them to help Flynn."

"Why didn't you ever say anything?"

Malakai smiled at Boston and shrugged. "It wasn't my place. I only found out a couple of weeks ago. I figure if one of them or Flynn wanted us to know, they'd tell us."

"Ah, smart and sexy," Flynn cooed. "Yeah, I'll definitely be keepin' ya."

Malakai just snorted. "Like you have a choice."

"We need to celebrate." Boston's skin tingled he was so happy. "How quick can your parents be here?" That part made him a little nervous since he'd still yet to meet Flynn's folks.

"Ya wantin' them to come?" Flynn sounded awed. Then he crushed Boston to him and attacked his mouth with enough enthusiasm to make the room spin. "Plan us a party, Boston Mackey, and I'll call my Ma and Da."

"It's the full moon in about five minutes," Boston said as he realized his skin tingling wasn't from only relief and happiness, but from his shifter trying to come to the surface. "Do you want to run, or should I take an Inhibitor?" Blaise had managed to perfect the Inhibitors without all the sexual side effects. Though he liked shifting and running through the woods, it was nice that he was no longer forced if he didn't feel like it.

"Can I go with you?" Malakai asked hesitantly.

"Of course!" Malakai never asked to run the fields or forests with them on the full moon. The idea made Boston's heart sing. "You can ride on Flynn's back...naked."

Malakai didn't even bat a lash. "Cool, but I have to be back before the sun comes up."

"I'll get ya home, sweet darlin'."

"Okay, then shoo." Malakai pushed them toward the patio doors. Once they'd moved into the main house, Stavion had given them a large suite on the first floor with easy outside access for just such occasions. "I don't want beasties in my nice, clean living room. I'll be out as soon as the sun sets." The second he'd finished speaking, there was a soft beep, signaling that the steel plates over the widows would be lifting in three minutes.

Boston waited for Malakai to exit the room before rushing over to the keypad on the wall and punching in the code to override the steel plates covering the patio doors.

Shrugging off their clothes, Boston felt like his skin was going to crawl off as he waited for the coverings to slide away. As soon as the metallic grinding and soft whirring stopped, he and Flynn racedthroughthe doors, barely making it outside before they began their shifts.

Boston dropped to his knees and panted as he felt the energy flowing through him. His body grew bigger, more powerful, and his soft white fur sprouted over his body. His hands and feet became hooves, his chest expanded, and his legs lengthened. When the transformation was complete, he looked over his white, furry shoulder, watching as the sun finally sank over the horizon.

Flynn bumped him with his massive flank then dipped his head to nuzzle against Boston's neck. *"Ya be stunnin', sweetheart. I love you."*

"Love you, too," Boston sent back, nuzzling against the big Irish Thoroughbred, but careful not to poke his mate's eye out with his antlers. Damn, Flynn was massive. Big and muscular with a chestnut coat and black mane that shone in the moonlight—he was breathtaking.

"Well, I love you guys, too. Can we go now?"

Boston snorted and pawed at the ground in approval when Malakai sashayed up to them, naked as the day he was born.

"Up ya go." Flynn bent one front leg and knelt low enough to the ground for Malakai to grab a hunk of his mane and hoist himself onto Flynn's back.

"This is so fucking cool." Malakai beamed down at Boston in excitement. "I'm so glad you guys like the nighttime better, because I don't think this would be as much fun during the day. People probably wouldn't like seeing my skinny ass."

"Your ass is perfect, baby. I love you."

"I'll take good care of ya when we come home, love. Then we'll do it all over again, when Boston finds his way back."

Boston shivered at the mental image of his mates joined together, their naked bodies slick with sweat as they moved as one. *"Take pictures."*

Malakai laughed, and Flynn made a horsey kind of snort. "I'll make sure you get lots of attention when you shift back."

Satisfied with the answer, Boston led them around the back of the house and across the field in a slow trot, enjoying Malakai's whoops and laughter, loving the way the wind blew his hair back from his angelic face.

Boston's life was perfect. His mates were everything he'd ever wanted, and adjusting his schedule around Malakai's inability to be out in the daylight had been a piece of cake. He still felt the need to feel the sunshine on his face occasionally, but he was happiest in the night.

If this is how his life would always be with his mates, he couldn't begrudge the dark. His sunlight came from the two men at his side. With them, he could face anything.

Slowing as they neared the tree line, Boston led his men through the lush forest and out the other side to an enormous field where they could run and play all night. Flynn shot past him, galloping at full speed as Malakai cheered him on and his laughter rang out through the night.

Boston just stood on the edge of the field and watched them, his heart swelling with love until he thought it would burst from his chest. They were his forever.

Their lives wouldn't be perfect. They'd argue, of course. Everyone did. There would be times when they needed their space, but he had no doubt they'd always find their way back to each other. Besides, making up was half the fun of fighting.

Sprinting across the field to join his loves, Boston knew his life would never be the same, and looked forward to the journey. Glancing up at the full moon as he ran, he couldn't help but smile internally.

Who needed the sun when his endless midnight was so much more fun?

THE END

WWW.GABRIELLEEVANS.COM

ABOUT THE AUTHOR

Gabrielle Evans grew up in a small town in southern Oklahoma. We are talking one red light that may or may not work depending on the day of the week. She married her high school sweetheart and the rest is pretty much history. They have two very active boys and one high-strung wiener dog that keeps her constantly on the go. For now, she parks her car in central Indiana, but who knows what tomorrow will bring.

Gabrielle believes in love at first sight, falling hard and fast, taking chances, and grabbing your happy-ever-after with both hands. Most importantly, she believes that a great cup of coffee can cure anything.

Also by Gabrielle Evans

Siren Classic ManLove: The Moonlight Breed 1:
Leap of Faith
Siren Classic ManLove: The Moonlight Breed 2:
By the Light of the Moon
Siren Classic ManLove: The Moonlight Breed 3:
Whispers in the Night
Ménage Amour ManLove: The Moonlight Breed 4:
Softly Spoken Lies

For all other titles, please visit
www.bookstrand.com/gabrielle-evans

Siren Publishing, Inc.
www.SirenPublishing.com

Lightning Source UK Ltd.
Milton Keynes UK
UKOW031810220312

189425UK00010B/80/P